LADY GUNSMITH

3

Roxy Doyle and The Shanghai Saloon

LADY GUNSMITH

3

Roxy Doyle and The Shanghai Saloon

J. R. Roberts

SPEAKING VOLUMES, LLC
NAPLES, FLORIDA
2017

Roxy Doyle and The Shanghai Saloon

Copyright © 2017 by Robert J. Randisi

ISBN 978-1-62815-725-3

PART ONE

Chapter One

San Francisco,
Roxy's present

This was not Roxy Doyle's first time in San Francisco. That had been about four years ago, when she was still trying to transition from young Roxy Doyle to Lady Gunsmith, a name and reputation she acquired after training with Clint Adams, the Gunsmith, and then standing with him in a gunfight. The newspapers jumped on the name, and she used it as an opportunity to grow up. She desperately wanted to leave the abusive life she had endured as a young girl living in Utah, behind her.

Now after spending weeks in Oregon, trying to track down her missing father being there, Roxy realized the rumor that brought her there had been just that, a rumor.

She'd been wandering south along the coast since then, until a telegram found its way to her where she was staying in a hotel in Seattle.

The telegram was from Clint Adams, asking Roxy to go to San Francisco and talk to a friend of his. Further, it said a room was being held for her in a Portsmouth Square Hotel called The Flamingo Rose.

Well, she owed Clint Adams and the telegram was all it took. She headed for San Francisco, even though her first trip there had been less than enjoyable—except for a few moments.

She rode in on a Mustang she'd bought while traveling around Oregon looking for Gavin Doyle. The telegram from Clint was in her pocket as she reined in her horse in front of the hotel.

She didn't know if there actually was a flower called a Flamingo Rose, but there, above the doorway of the hotel, right next to the name was a big, pink rose. It was horrible.

She entered the hotel and approached the front desk, while a young clerk in his twenties watched and fell in love. There were more roses on the walls, mostly paintings of them, and even some on the overstuffed lobby furniture. A lot of money had been spent on the lobby, but then this was Portsmouth Square, home to a wide variety of hotels and gambling halls. They each had to strive to offer something unique.

But pink roses?

"Can I . . . help you, Miss?" he asked, anxiously.

"Yes, I believe you're holding a room for me," she said.

"Well," he said, "I hope so. I mean, er, what's your name?"

"Roxy Doyle."

"Ah yes, Miss Doyle," he said, brightening, "I was told to watch for you."

"Told by who?"

"My boss."

"And who's that?"

"His name is Anthony Tunkin."

"Tunkin? That's an odd name."

"Don't tell him that," the young man said. He turned and took a key off a hook. "I can walk you up, if you like?"

3

"No, I'm fine," she said. "I just have my saddlebags and rifle."

"Outside on your horse?"

"Yes."

"I'll get them!" He started around the desk, but she stopped him.

"Relax," she said. "I can get them myself. You'll just have to direct me to a livery stable where I can board my horse."

"That's no problem," he said. "I can even walk you there!"

"You're very kind," she said, "but I can do it myself. I just need directions."

"Sure thing. You go out—"

"Let's wait until I've put my things in my room and I come back down, okay?"

"Sure, Miss Doyle."

She went back outside to remove her saddlebags and rifle from her saddle. People passing—men, women, and some couples—turned to stare at her, something she was used to, by now. In the beginning people stared at her because of her startling beauty. Later, she was never sure if it was that, or the fact that they recognized her as Lady Gunsmith.

She re-entered the hotel, walked to the stairs and up to the second floor, found her room halfway down the hall. The inside resembled the lobby, with the same kind of furnishings, and the same paintings of pink roses on the walls.

She set her rifle and saddlebags down on the bed and walked to the window, saw that it looked out onto a side alley, not the front of the building. That suited her. The building was sheer, with no balconies or ledges.

The bed seemed comfortable, and even beckoned to her, but she had things to do. Her horse needed to be boarded, and then she needed a bath, a drink and a meal—not necessarily in that order.

She decided to talk to the helpful young desk clerk to try to arrange for all three.

Chapter Two

Within the next two hours Roxy was bathed, and fed, and her horse was taken care of. She came out of the hotel dining room—which was the fanciest place she had ever eaten in—and didn't quite know what came next.

The last thing Clint Adams' telegram said was that she was to check into the Flamingo Rose Hotel. There was nothing after that. She assumed that someone would be contacting her, but she didn't know how or when that would happen.

She wasn't quite dressed for Portsmouth Square nightlife, but then it wasn't night time, yet, so she decided to go for a walk.

As she reached the center of activity there were large hotel/gambling halls, and people crowding the streets, wearing their fanciest finery, on their way for a night's feast of drink, food and risk. Roxy found herself wishing she had a beautiful gown she could put on and wear into one of those places, like the Parker House, the Bella Union, the Aquila de Oro, the Varsouvienne, the Alhambra, the El Dorado Gambling Saloon, and many others.

As she watched people pass, and enter the saloons and halls, she remembered her last time there which had been only 4 years ago, but seemed a lot longer. She had felt so much younger, then. The problem was, she had matured by leaps and bounds, with all the adventures she'd had over the past 4 years. Now she was experiencing San Francisco and Portsmouth Square as a whole other person.

She left the Square and walked back to her hotel which, although referred to as a Portsmouth Square hotel, was really on the outer fringes of the action.

As she entered the hotel, wishing she didn't have to just sit in her room and wait for somebody to contact her, the young desk clerk excitedly waved to get her attention.

"*I* have a message here for you." He was holding an envelope in his hand.

"It wasn't here when I checked in?"

"No, Ma'am," he said, "it just came in within the past half hour."

She took the envelope from him. It had her name written on the front.

"Who brought it?"

"A messenger."

"So a reply isn't necessary?"

"I guess not," he said. "He didn't wait."

"Okay, thank you."

Instead of going to her room to read it she took it to one of the lobby chairs and sat down.

It read:

Dear Miss Doyle,

I am sorry not to have been there to greet you at the hotel. Please meet me for breakfast at 8 a.m.

tomorrow morning at Delmonico's and I will explain everything. And, of course, I appreciate Clint Adams' efforts to put us together.

Best,
Robert Pinkerton

She refolded the paper and replaced it in the envelope. She knew that Robert Pinkerton was one of Allan Pinkerton's sons. She knew Clint Adams had a history with the Pinkertons, and while it was not an acrimonious one, it wasn't something anyone would call friendly. For Clint to arrange a meeting must have meant he agreed the situation was serious. He was, however, leaving the final decision of what to do entirely up to her. His telegram never said he actually wanted her to accept the offer that was coming.

While training under the tutelage of the Gunsmith, Clint Adams had told her many stories. One was about working in the Intelligence Service during the Civil War as a very young man, under Major E.J. Allen, who was actually Allan Pinkerton. She also knew that Pinkerton had two sons, William and Robert, who he took into the agency.

So she was to meet his youngest son, Robert, for breakfast in the morning. Thankfully, she wouldn't have to wait around for days before finding out what this was all about.

She thought about going to one of the large gambling halls in the Square but decided against it for two reasons. One, she didn't have that gown she would have needed and two, she didn't gamble.

The fact was, she didn't know how to gamble. Faro, poker, blackjack, they were all a mystery to her. Clint Adams' teachings were designed to help her stay alive, and had never included gambling.

Perhaps, if she did have proper attire, she would go and find herself a young man—or an older one—who would take her under his wing and teach her, but that would have to wait. If she accepted Pinkerton's offer, she'd be spending some more time in San Francisco, and maybe she could think about shopping and gambling then.

And, if that offer included some kind of work, she might never have time to learn to gamble.

In truth, however, she'd been gambling with her life ever since she left home at 15 years of age. And, at least for 10 years, she'd been on a winning streak.

She was still alive.

Chapter Three

Robert Allan Pinkerton arose at 6 a.m. that morning to ready himself for his meeting with the Lady Gunsmith. He was pleased that, while his father was out chasing the James boys, he had left his older brother, William, in charge of their Chicago office, while sending Robert—the youngest son—to San Francisco to open the office, there.

No sooner had he arrived, the Pinkerton Agency had accepted a case that, for months, had been baffling them. Several men had been sent into the field to investigate, and had disappeared. It was then that Robert contracted Clint Adams.

He knew that the Gunsmith and his father, the famed Allan Pinkerton, were not on good terms. That stemmed from the Gunsmith's refusal—on several occasions—to join the Pinkerton Agency. Robert's father did not take rejection well. However, Adams had, from time to time, agreed to work with the Pinkertons on a case when it interested him. This one did not interest him, but his response to Robert's telegram did mention someone who might be—Roxy Doyle, who the newspapers were now calling Lady Gunsmith.

Robert immediately took to the idea. The missing agents had all been men. Perhaps it was time to send a woman in where men had not been able to do the job. He knew his older brother would probably not agree with him, so he didn't let them in on his decision. And he wouldn't, at least, not until he managed to secure her participation. But his father had hired

Kate Warne—the very first Lady Pinkerton Agent—back in 1853, and then Hattie Lewis in 1860 and Elizabeth Baker in 1861. He had also used Baker in his Intelligence Service during the Civil War.

"Women could be most useful in worming out secrets in many places which would be impossible for a male detective," he had heard his father say. But he still wouldn't let the old man know about Lady Gunsmith until later. Right now, this was his call, and his alone, to make.

Robert got himself dressed, checking the mirror before leaving his rented house. His wife, Anna Elizabeth, was still back in Chicago, so he'd have to straighten his own tie and collar for a while. When he thought he was presentable he donned his bowler hat, and left to walk to Delmonico's, and his early morning meeting with Roxy Doyle.

***

Pinkerton was already seated at a table when Roxy arrived. He stood as a maitre d' showed her to the table. She was surprised to find that he was a tall, handsome young man, only four or five years older than she was. Roxy was tall, but as she reached him she saw that he had a few inches on her.

"Miss Doyle?" he asked.

"That's right," she said.

"I'm so pleased you could make it." He shook hands with her like a man, not handling hers like it was fragile.

11

"Please, sit." She knew when men looked at her they thought two things. One, she was beautiful, and two, she was definitely not fragile.

He waited until she had seated herself, with the help of the maître d', and then sat back down.

"I ordered coffee," he said, indicating the pot on the table. "I hope that was all right."

"That's fine," she said, studying his face. He looked both refined and intelligent. He did not look freshly shaved, but there was no hint of stubble. She wondered if he was one of those men who only had to shave once or twice a week?

He picked up the pot and asked, "May I?"

"Please." She liked his manners. She was used to dealing with men who had none, at all.

He poured coffee for both of them, and set the pot down. She was further impressed by the fact that he had not had a cup while waiting.

"I hope this is all right for breakfast?" he asked, indicating the restaurant.

"It's fine, Mr. Pinkerton."

"Please," he said, "I'd like you to call me Robert."

"That's fine . . . Robert," she said "and you can call me Roxy. But maybe now we can stop being so polite and get down to why I'm here?"

"I'm sorry," he apologized, "I thought we'd order, first, but if you'd rather—"

"No," she said, "I'm the one who's sorry. I'm not used to men with manners. Forgive me. Yes, let's order."

She suddenly found herself intimidated by him. He was obviously very educated. Most of her education had come from her own experiences and observations since leaving Utah 10 years ago. Would he see through the facade she'd built up for herself?

A waiter came over to take their order. She avoided the steak-and-eggs she might have chosen, and instead simply ordered ham-and-eggs. She didn't think sawing into an inch thick steak with a steak knife would be ladylike enough for this breakfast meeting. He went the same way, after allowing her to order, first.

"There," he said, "now we can talk. Is your hotel all right?"

"It's fine."

"I didn't know if you were a gambler, so rather than pluck you down right in the middle of the action, I thought we'd simply put you walking distance from it."

"Actually, I don't gamble," she said, "but I have nothing against it. I've just . . . never had the time."

"Really?" he said. "perhaps, while you're here, you'll let me show you around, then. Perhaps give you some pointers?"

"That would be . . . nice," she said, "but that's really not why I'm here, is it?"

"No, of course not," he said. "All right, then, to business. The Pinkerton Agency would like you to act as one of our agents, at least temporarily."

"So you're not offering me a job, then?"

"A temporary position," he said, "which you will, of course, be paid for. But no, not a permanent one. Though that could come later, if it seems appropriate."

"Let's just stick to the business at hand, then. Do you know why Clint suggested me for this job?"

"Well," Pinkerton said, "first of all, he didn't want it. And second, when he knew what the job was, he thought that a woman might make more sense. After some thought, I agreed."

"Is that odd?" she asked. "A Pinkerton agreeing with Clint Adams?"

He smiled, showing perfect teeth. "Ah, I see you know our checkered history."

"Clint told me a thing or two about him and your father."

"Yes, my father was quite impressed with Clint's service during the war. He was very disappointed when he was turned down after offering Clint a position with the agency."

"And your father holds a grudge."

"Uh, well, yes, he's been known to."

"So why isn't he here offering me this job?" she asked.

"Right now my father is a little occupied with the James boys. My older brother is running the Chicago office, and I'm out here handling things."

"And there's something you haven't been handling?" she asked.

He frowned at that, and she immediately felt bad.

"I'm sorry, I didn't mean—"

"No, no, that's fine," he said. "The fact is we have been having trouble with this one, and a woman's perspective might be exactly what we need."

"And don't you have any women on your staff?"

"Not at the present time, no," he said. "Adams said he thought you were eminently qualified for this, though."

"Well," she said, "let me hear what the job is, and then we can decide that . . . together."

Chapter Four

"Forgive me," he said, "but I'm not sure how much you know about San Francisco."

"I was here once before," she said.

"Very well," he said, "then you know about the Barbary Coast."

"I know some, but educate me."

"The Barbary Coast is pretty much the opposite of Portsmouth Square. That makes it ironic that Pacific Street actually runs from the Square right down to the Coast. Both places offer pretty much the same things, there's just a . . . difference in quality. While the establishments in Portsmouth Square offer fine dining and the classiest forms of gambling and entertainment, the Barbary Coast features saloons, gambling halls and brothels that feature pickpockets, prostitutes, flim-flam artists, female impersonators—"

"Female impersonators?"

"Oh yes, the Barbary Coast caters to a very homosexual community. Many men have paid to spend time with a lady, only to find when the petticoats come off, that they're with a man. And some of them prefer it that way."

Roxy had not had many experiences with homosexuals, beyond occasionally being propositioned by another woman, mostly in saloons.

"I hope you're not going to ask me to impersonate a female impersonator."

"No, no, nothing like that," he said. "Besides, anyone can look at you and know that you're all woman." She was surprised when he suddenly blushed and stammered. "Oh, I'm sorry, that was . . . unprofessional . . . I didn't mean . . ."

"That's fine, Robert," she said. "You didn't say anything offensive."

The waiter came with their plates, momentarily saving Robert Pinkerton from his embarrassment.

They took a few moments to make inroads into their breakfast, then sat back and regarded each other.

"Do you mind if we keep talking while we eat?" he asked.

"I prefer it," she said.

He nodded, wiped his mouth with his cloth napkin, then put it back in his lap.

"There's an epidemic on the Barbary Coast," he said.

"An illness?"

"A plague of sorts," he said. "Do you know what it means to be shanghaied?"

"Yes, I've heard the term," she said. "Men being kidnapped, forced to work as part of a ship's crew?"

"That's exactly it. It's also called crimping."

"If there's such an epidemic on the Barbary Coast, why isn't the law involved?"

"Because it's not against the law."

"What?"

"It's true," he said. "There's no law on the books that prohibits crimping."

"So who's your client?" she asked, after swallowing a bite of ham-and-eggs.

"There's a newly formed group called the Barbary Coast Dockworkers Association."

"Why are the dockworkers concerned about it?"

"Well, for one thing," he said, "some of their men have been shanghaied. For another, many dockworkers are being blamed for it."

"So they're getting blamed on both sides?" she asked. "That hardly seems fair."

"They agree," Pinkerton said. "That's why they asked us to do something about it."

"What can you do?" she asked.

"Well," he said, "it's generally considered to be one man who's responsible for all the crimping, sort of like Joseph 'Bunco' Kelly was in Portland during the seventies."

"Bunco?"

"Yes," Pinkerton laughed. "He was called that after he sold a cigar store wooden Indian to a ship's captain for fifty dollars. The man didn't realize he didn't have a real body until he was at sea. And then there was Shanghai Kelly and Shanghai Chicken Devine, who were doing the same things right here some years back."

"Could they be responsible again?"

"We don't think so," he said. "There's been no indication that either of them are back in business."

"So this is somebody new."

"Yes," he said, "and we want to find him. So far we've sent three men in, and they've disappeared."

"Dead?" she asked.

"Or simply shanghaied, themselves. I'd prefer that, actually. Means they'll come walking back into the office at some point in the future."

"And tell you who shanghaied them," she pointed out.

"We can't wait that long," he said. "We need to find the culprit, and soon."

"Is there a time limit?"

He put his fork down and sat back. "The simple answer to that is, we need a win. You see, Jesse and Frank James have been frustrating my father for months. If he doesn't capture them it's going to be considered a black mark on the agency's name. I need to get us a victory."

"Do you have any idea where these ships are going once they leave port?" she asked.

"Probably to Alaska," he said. "There are a lot of ships carrying supplies to the Klondike."

She wasn't asking these questions so much because she was curious, as she wanted some time to think. Was this something she wanted to get involved in? And she still didn't know exactly what he wanted her to do.

Maybe she should find out.

Chapter Five

"Okay, then," she said, putting down her fork, "what exactly do you want me to do?"

"Go undercover," he said.

She knew the Pinkerton Agency had a reputation for doing business this way, like when they broke up the Molly Maguires during the coal miners strikes of the 1870's, by putting a man undercover. This, however, was not a strike.

"If it's not against the law," she said, "what will you do when you find the man?"

"Expose him," Pinkerton said, "take steps to force him to leave San Francisco."

"How would you do that?"

"You're putting the cart before the horse, Roxy," he said. "First we've got to find him."

"Right," she said. "So you don't want me to be a female impersonator. What then? A prostitute? My pickpocketing skills are poor."

"Nothing like that," he said. "I don't think this will be very hard for you. I want you to go in as a saloon girl. You'll obviously look very good in a bright colored gown, and men will approach you, start a conversation with you."

"That's all you want me to do? Talk?"

"And listen," he said. "You might hear somcthing during the course of a shift."

"Do you have a saloon picked out?"

"Yes," he said, "in fact, we think we have the very saloon in mind where most of the crimping is taking place. "It's the Blue Lady Saloon and Gambling Hall. Inside the agency we're referring to it as 'the Shanghai Saloon.'"

"The Shanghai Saloon," she repeated. "I like that better than the real name."

"So what do you say?"

"Am I just supposed to apply for a job there?"

"Some of the saloon owners have joined in with the dock workers to pay our fees. But I think it would look better if you went in and applied."

"What if I don't get the job?"

"I can't see why they wouldn't hire you," he said. "I mean, after seeing you all decked out."

"Decked out?"

"You know," he said, waving a hand in front of his face, "made up."

She sat back, feeling somewhat flummoxed.

"I'm really not very good . . . I mean, I don't use a lot—"

"And I can see why," he said, "you really don't need it, do you?" he pushed on before he embarrassed himself, again. "But I think in this case you'll have to use it . . . I mean, you've seen how saloon girls look . . ."

Her experience with make-up was negligible. She was afraid she'd end up making herself look like a clown.

"I don't think I can—"

"We have someone who can help you with that," he said, quickly.

"Oh?"

"Yes, she's had a lot of experience with beauty products and, in fact, will soon be embarking on a stage career," Pinkerton said.

Roxy still hadn't made her final decision, but that bit of information was helpful.

"Oh," Roxy said, "well, if you've got someone who can help me . . . who is it?"

"I don't know if you've ever heard of her," Robert said. "She's a friend of my father's. An actress. Her name is Sarah Bernhardt."

***

Of course she had heard of Sarah Bernhardt. She was probably the most famous actress in the world.

But she said calmly, "Yes, I've heard of her."

Pinkerton didn't push for a decision while they finished their breakfast, but after the plates were cleared and they each had a fresh cup of coffee he said, "So what do you think?"

"I must admit, having Miss Bernhardt help me with my make-up could be a decision maker."

"Don't forget she's an actress," Pinkerton said. "She can help you with playing your part, as well."

"That's true."

"And if it's the money, we can pay you—"

"It's not the money," she said, "although that will be nice." Roxy's only struggle in the search for her father—aside from the frustration of following up rumors—was struggling to make enough money to keep herself going. A Pinkerton paycheck would go a long way toward financing her for a while.

"All right," she said, "let's say I agree to do this. When do we start?"

"Miss Bernhardt will be here tomorrow," Pinkerton said. "She's diverting just slightly from her American tour to help us. Once we've got your make-up and hair right, and you think you're ready to play the part, you can go and apply for a job the following day."

"That's fast."

"Well . . . I'm eager to get this one taken care of."

"I hope I'm the one to do it for you," she said. "All right, let's give this a try."

"Excellent!" His smile lit up the room. "I would like to take you to dinner tonight to celebrate, but . . ."

"But?"

"It might not do for us to be seen together now that you've agreed—I know," he said, as something occurred to him. "I'm renting a house. Why don't you come to dinner there, tonight?"

"You're going to cook?" she asked, surprised.

"Oh, no," he said, "my wife is the cook, but she's in Chicago. No, I'll have the dinner brought in from outside. Waiters and everything. What do you say?"

"Sounds all right with me," she said.

"As long as you don't mind coming to my home, that is," he added.

"Well, you did say there would be waiters," she said, "and . . ."

"And?" he asked.

She smiled and said, "I'll have my gun."

Chapter Six

Robert Pinkerton and Roxy agreed to leave Delmonico's separately.

"It's bad enough we could have been seen here, together," he said. "Let's not take any more chances. Last thing we want is somebody who had breakfast here seeing you at the Shanghai Saloon."

"Agreed."

As she started to rise he stopped her, reached into his pocket and came out with his wallet. They had agreed on her fee, but she hadn't expected him to pay now.

"Here is some expense money," he said. "You'll need to buy some dresses and . . . other products. You'll also need to move to a more . . . ordinary hotel. We wouldn't want anyone wondering why you're working in a Barbary Coast saloon and living in a Portsmouth Square hotel."

She accepted the money he handed her and asked, "Any suggestions for a hotel?"

"Wait until you get the job," he said. "It may come with a room in the building. If not, ask them to recommend a place."

"Okay."

He allowed her to leave first, ordering another pot of coffee from the waiter. He was impressed by his first meeting with her, but he hoped that Roxy Doyle was the person Clint Adams thought she was.

***

Outside, Roxy stopped and took a deep breath. The day was clear, with a stiff, Fall breeze in the air. This would be just the first of a succession of different days, for her.

She didn't know if she was making the right decision, but at least it would be a respite from the search for her father. If Gavin Doyle was out there somewhere, he'd have to wait a little bit longer for his daughter to find him.

***

Rex Burns walked through his Blue Lady Saloon and Gambling Hall which, at this early hour, was closed. Woodbury, his bartender, was sweeping up some of the remnants of the previous night's festivities. Not that his customers worried about coming in and getting dirty. They pretty much brought the Barbary Coast dirt in with them, and left it behind when they departed.

As much as Burns would have liked to own an establishment in Portsmouth Square, he really didn't mind having one of the most popular places on the Barbary Coast. The place was packed every night, and his side business was bringing him a lot of income.

"'mornin', boss," Woodbury said.

"'mornin', Wood."

Wood was an ex-boxer who also served as a bouncer. The regular customers had learned not to mess with him, and new customers found it out pretty damn quick if they started a fuss. Woodbury had the free hand to break any head he needed to break to keep or restore order. Some customers liked to start in with him because he was black, but Burns didn't care what color he was, as long as he got the job done.

Wood stopped sweeping and asked, "Want some coffee, boss?"

"Yeah, thanks."

The bartender nodded, set the broom aside, went behind the bar and poured his boss a mug of strong coffee.

"How's business?" Burns asked him.

Wood knew that Burns was very well aware of how business was, but this was their morning ritual.

"B'iness could always be better, boss, you knows that."

"Yep, I knows that," Burns said.

Wood usually lapsed into his nigger talk when the front door opened. Other than that, he spoke in the cadence of an educated man. He was a smart man inside the ring and out, and as well as being the bartender and bouncer, he often served as manager when Burns wasn't around.

"How are the girls?" Burns asked.

"They puttin' out when they wants to, boss," Wood said, "and they doin' their jobs on the floor."

"That's fine."

The saloon girls and whores came and went, but the group that Burns had working for him now was an adequate one. Although there was always room for another good girl.

Or not-so-good girl.

Wood came around the bar and picked up the broom again.

"We've got to get somebody else to do that for you, Wood," Burns observed.

"I'm fine, boss," Wood said. "Keeps me relaxed."

Burns knew Wood was the most relaxed man he'd ever met, but when the front doors opened, he was ready to go.

The worst mistake a customer could make was thinking that Woodbury Jefferson was a slow movin', slow talkin' nigger.

"I'll be in my office, Wood," Burns said, taking his coffee mug with him.

"I'll be openin' soon, boss," Wood said. "We should have a good day."

"Yeah," Burns said, "we should."

As he walked across the floor to his office he exchanged nods with his other employees, as they were uncovering their tables. Before long the sound of a roulette wheel would be constant, as would the noises from the Faro, Blackjack and dice tables. But his favorite sound was the one the big Wheel of Fortune made as it went round and round, because it was his fortune the wheel was making.

It was his fortune all the tables were making and, except for his side business, he had no partners. The Blue Lady was all his.

Should've named it something else, though. Damned woman he was keeping company with when he christened it, and now he was stuck with it.

Chapter Seven

Roxy did her shopping, and enjoyed herself while doing it. She didn't buy much, though. Once she got the job—and she wasn't as confident as Robert Pinkerton that she would—they would probably tell her what kind of dresses to buy. And although she had been out of her element, she enjoyed shopping for the cosmetics she'd need for her saloon girl look.

Returning from the day of seeing the San Francisco stores, she had another bath for herself before dressing for dinner at Robert Pinkerton's house. She decided to simply wear clean trail clothes, and strapped her gun on before leaving. She had already been recognized enough on the streets of western towns to know that she wouldn't be safe walking without her gun. It was something Clint Adams had tried to drill into her, and it was something she had ultimately learned for herself.

Out in front of the hotel she flagged down a passing horse drawn cab. The driver was so eager to pick her up he dropped down to the ground and smiled at her.

"Where to, Ma'am?"

She gave him the address Pinkerton had given her.

"I know where that is," he said. "Near Nob Hill. Fancy. Hop in."

He held his hand out and assisted her into the back of his cab, then scrambled into his seat, grabbed his whip, and away they went.

***

When they reached the house, the driver jumped down again and helped her from the cab.

"Can I do anything else for you?" he asked, after she paid him.

"Yes," she said. "Come back for me in three hours."

"Three hours," he said. "You've got it. My name's Ted." He put his hand out and she shook it.

"Roxy," she said. "See you in three hours."

"I'll be here."

The house was two stories, with gabled, shingled rooftops, and bay windows on the second floor. As she approached the front door she heard the cab drive away behind her. The door opened before she reached it, and Robert Pinkerton appeared in the doorway.

"Welcome to my temporary home," he said.

"Thank you."

She entered and he closed the door. The inside was warm, and she could smell two things—food, and him.

"Dinner's almost ready," he said. "Would you like a glass of wine?"

"Sure."

He led her to a living room that was expensively but impersonally furnished.

"This isn't you," she said, while he poured two glasses of red wine.

"You're right," he said, handing her a glass. "I rented it already furnished."

"You mean the Agency rented it."

"That's right," he said, "just like the Agency bought you some clothes today. Am I right?"

"Some," she said. "I decided to wait until I have the job to finish my shopping."

"Probably a good idea," he said. "They'll tell you what to wear." He held his glass up to her. "To success."

"Success," she said, clinking glasses. They drank. "Something smells good."

"Have you ever had Beef Wellington?" he asked.

"I have no idea what that is."

"You'll love it. Come."

He led her to the dining room, where a table was set with a white tablecloth and two chairs.

"Sit," he said, holding a chair out for her.

She walked to the table, started to sit in the chair.

"Do you always wear your gun to dinner?" he asked.

"Always," she said.

"Well," he said, "I suppose that's the price you have to pay for having a reputation."

"One of them," she said, sitting. In front of her was a large, china plate, and expensive looking silverware.

He went around to the other side of the table, sat, picked up a silver bell from the table and rang it. Immediately, two waiters appeared, presumably from the kitchen, carrying serving trays.

As they ladled and spooned food onto the plates she said to Pinkerton, "It looks like you went all out."

"I'm only trying to impress a lady. This food is from Vincent's," he said. "One of the finest restaurants in San Francisco.

"I haven't been called a lady in a while," she said. "But as you say, that's one of the costs of a reputation."

"Do you hold it against Clint Adams?" he asked.

"Hold what against him?"

"Isn't he the reason you're called Lady Gunsmith?"

"Not at all," she said. "All he did was make sure I didn't get killed the first time I faced somebody with a gun. The rest is all me."

He nodded.

"Oh, and the newspapers, of course," she said. "Once they christened me, it got around."

"I see."

"So this is Beef Wellington?" she asked.

"It is."

She cut into her food, saw that the pastry on her plate was actually covering a beautiful piece of beef. She tried it, and nodded her head.

"It's wonderful," she said.

"I'm glad you like it."

"So what about you?" she asked.

"What about me?"

"You and your brother," she said. "William?"

"That's right."

"You both have to live up to your father's reputation, don't you?"

"Oh, definitely," he said. "And living up to his, will probably keep either one of us from forging our own."

"Does that bother you?"

"Not right now," he said, "but who knows what will happen in the years to come?"

"What do you expect to happen in years to come?" she asked.

"Maybe we'll all go our own ways," he suggested. "I know my brother has his own plans."

"And you?"

"Not yet," he said. "I'm too busy being the good little son, at the moment."

"You seem to be your own man," she said.

"Thank you," he said, "I like to think that I am."

"How does your, uh, wife feel about all of this?" she asked.

"She wanted to come, of course," he said, "but I told her I'd be working all the time. Do you know what she said?"

"That she'd be shopping all the time?"

He laughed. "Exactly! So I told her, no, stay home and shop in Chicago."

"I'll bet that didn't sit well with her."

"She was angry to beat the band," Pinkerton said, "but what can you do? I'm here to work, and I don't need any added distractions." He stared across the table at her. "That is, any more than I have, at the moment."

This time he didn't blush when he said something nice to her, so she figured he was flirting on purpose, now. She found him attractive enough. It was too bad he was married.

"This beef is very good," she said.

"And there's plenty more."

Chapter Eight

They talked more about the Pinkerton family as they ate. When he tried to get her to talk about her family, she deflected. Why tell him about any of the abuse of her childhood—a childhood that ended at 15, when she left Utah and started the search for her father.

Over desert, an excellent apple cobbler, and coffee, he said, "Clint Adams didn't tell us much about you. Well, there wasn't much room in a telegram. All he said was that you'd get the job done."

"I'm flattered by his confidence."

"And since you're not being very forthcoming with your history tonight," he went on, "all I know about you is what I've read."

"In newspapers."

"And reports."

"Reports?"

"Well," he said, "I had to have you checked out before I considered offering you this job."

"You're offering it to me?" she asked. "I thought you were asking me to take it."

"Yes, well, that's true enough—"

"I don't know if I like that there's a report on me," she said. "I wouldn't think it would be any more accurate than the newspaper accounts."

"Then why don't you tell me something that's accurate?" he suggested. "I mean, since we're going to be working to-gether."

She remained silent for the moment.

"For one thing, I've heard that you're looking for your father," he said. "Is that accurate?"

Grudgingly, she said, "Yes."

"And you've been looking for . . . how many years, now?"

"Ten."

"Wow. Do you really think he's still out there, some-where?" he asked.

"There are . . . stories, rumors."

"About Gavin Doyle, the bounty hunter, right?"

"That's right."

"Yes, I've heard the rumors."

"Which ones?"

"Both," he said. "About him being dead, and about him being alive."

"Have you heard anything about where he is?"

"No," Pinkerton said, "I can't say I have. But I tell you what I can do."

"What?"

"When this job is over, I can start looking into it," he said. "See if we can't find something more solid than rumors for you."

"You'd do that for me?"

"Why not?" Pinkerton said. "You're helping me out, aren't you?"

"You're paying me."

"That's beside the point," he said. "You could have said no and ridden out of here tomorrow."

What was the main reason she was saying yes? A brief respite from the search for her father? Not wanting to disappoint Clint Adams? This was now probably the best reason of all. Do this job for the Pinkerton Agency, and then have them find her father for her.

"Well, I'm committed now," she said.

"Good," Pinkerton said. "Why don't we go into the library for some brandy?"

Brandy was not a drink Roxy normally indulged in, but then neither was red wine, so she said, "Let's."

She followed him down the hall to a room where all the walls were lined with books.

"Now I would believe this was yours," she said.

"Sadly, it's not," he said. "This was also here when I rented the house."

He walked to a sideboard and poured two glasses of brandy.

"I know this all feels very fancy," he said, "red wine, Beef Wellington, now brandy, but I really am just trying to impress you."

"Well," she lied, "you have."

"Good."

She walked around the room looking at the spines of the books. She didn't recognize many, but the ones she did were fiction, the works of writers like Mark Twain and Charles Dickens.

"I had an idea for tonight," Pinkerton said.

37

"What was that?"

"I thought we might go out to some of the gambling halls in Portsmouth Square, after all."

"And risk being seen together?"

"Well," he said, "I thought that you might go in disguise."

She turned away from the shelves and looked at him.

"Disguised as what?"

"Not what," he said. "Who. And just as . . . well, somebody else"

"And how would I do that?"

"Well, upstairs in one of the bedrooms are some dresses . . . and a black wig."

"A wig," she said. "Hmmm . . ."

"I could show you some gambling, and you would see some of the beautiful people in the high-class saloons and halls. Although I'm sure none of them would be as beautiful as you."

Now he was just blatantly flirting. She thought it wouldn't be a bad thing to have Robert Pinkerton dangling on the end of her hook.

"Why don't I go upstairs and have a look?" she suggested.

Chapter Nine

Pinkerton showed Roxy to the upstairs bedroom in question, then closed the door, leaving her alone in the room. She saw the black wig on a dressing table, then opened the closet to find it filled with brightly colored dresses. She wondered if Pinkerton had gone shopping for her, or if the dresses had also come with the house. She also wondered who actually owned it, and how Robert Pinkerton had come to rent the place.

She had no trouble choosing a dress that would fit in with the Portsmouth Square crowd. After all, they were all lovely. The wig was a little trickier. She had never worn one before, and had some trouble getting her mass of red hair pinned underneath it. By the time she was done she thought she looked ridiculous, and would never have left the house looking that way. The gown—an off the shoulder, royal blue number with a daring neckline—was not a problem, but that wig!

Besides, she didn't think that, with her skin tone she made a very good brunette.

She was standing in front of the mirror, turning this way and that, when he knocked on the door.

"May I come in?"

"Why not?" she called out. "Nothing good is happening in here."

He opened the door and entered, regarded her as she turned to face him.

"You look beautiful in that dress," he said.

"It's the wig," she said. "I've never worn one before. I can't get my hair under it, and it's the wrong color for my skin."

"That's true," he said, approaching her. "And you do have beautiful skin."

Up close he had that look and scent of a man in heat. Married or not, he was going to try to kiss her. Maybe even more. She could feel it. She wasn't sure how she should handle the situation. Usually, she dominated when it came to this, but did she want to dominate him? She was going to work for him, and then she hoped he was going to help her find her father. The last thing she wanted to do was humiliate him, or even cause him the slightest embarrassment. How would he take it if she turned him down because he was married?

"Maybe," he said, putting his hands on either side of the wig, "you should just take it off."

He plucked it from her head, set it aside, then went to work unpinning her hair so that it fell to her shoulders.

"There," he said, "that's so much better."

He backed up a few steps to regard her again.

"So?"

"Beautiful," he said, "but we can't go out with you looking that way, and we don't have another way of disguising you."

"That's all right," she said. "I'll learn to gamble another time."

"I'm sorry," he said.

"Whose dresses are these?" she asked. "Whose room?"

"The people who own the house are acquaintances of mine," he explained. "They're traveling in Europe, and made the house available to us."

"For rent?"

Pinkerton shrugged.

"It's only fair," he said, "and as you pointed out, the Agency is paying. I'll leave you alone so you can take the gown off."

He headed for the door.

"Wait."

He turned.

She reached behind her, undid the dress, and tugged it down so that it fell to her feet. She didn't have the right kind of support garments to wear beneath it, so she was completely naked. She took a deep breath, knowing from experience what that did to her full breasts.

Pinkerton stared at her, and she could see him taking in every curve, every nuance of her body.

But that was all. He didn't move.

"Was I wrong?" she asked.

He opened his mouth to speak, but nothing came out. He had to lick his lips before trying to speak again.

"No," he said, "you weren't wrong."

Now he moved toward her, and she knew she had him. After this, he'd make sure the Pinkertons would use all their resources to locate her father. And she needed this, before she went to the Barbary Coast and became someone else in the Shanghai Saloon.

***

Robert Pinkerton thought briefly of his wife back in Chicago. But this was a decision he had made at dinner—and probably before. He already knew that Roxy Doyle was a remarkable woman of uncommon beauty. And now, with her standing before him, naked, offering herself to him, what other decision was there for him to make, but this one.

He walked to her, his hands shaking slightly, took her into his arms, and kissed her.

Chapter Ten

Roxy allowed Robert Pinkerton to take her hand and lead her from the room, down the hall to his room. But before going out the door, she reached over and grabbed her gunbelt.

He turned as they entered his room, saw her with the gunbelt slung over her naked shoulder, and found the scene both hypnotic and erotic.

"That gun really does go everywhere with you, doesn't it?" he asked.

"Everywhere!" she confirmed.

His bed had a thick, wooden headboard, but there was a post for her to hang the gunbelt from. That done, she turned to face him.

"You're still dressed," she said.

"Yes," he said, "but we can take care of that."

He undid his tie and started to unbutton his shirt as she approached him and undid his belt. In moments they had him naked, a long and hard penis jutting up from between slender thighs.

"Oh my," she said, because she knew men liked to hear it. He did have a nice penis, but she was not in any danger of losing control of herself.

He, on the other hand, didn't seem to be able to control the twitching motion of his hands. It was as if he didn't know where to grab her first. Although he was married, she began to wonder just how experienced he was in this kind of situation.

So she decided to take control.

She reached down, grasped him by the penis and gently tugged him toward the bed. Turning him, she pulled the bed sheets down and pushed him onto the mattress.

She got on the bed and straddled him. His chest was completely smooth, not a hint of hair. She reached down and scraped the nails of both hands across his chest, leaving red marks behind. His breathing quickened. His cock was trapped beneath her, and her pussy was getting wet, so she rubbed herself up and down the length of him, anointing him with her juices. When she had him good and wet she lifted her hips and took him inside of her.

She sighed as she sat down on him, closing her eyes. She was always surprised at how this simple act excited her, yet relaxed her at the same time.

Pressing both hands down on his sternum she began to ride him up and down, enjoying the sound of his grunts and groans when she came down on him. She had considered taking him into her mouth, but she had the feeling he was more traditional than that. It would either overexcite him, or make him feel dirty. All she wanted right now was a little gratification for herself, and a way to keep him on the hook. Robert Pinkerton was not her type, but he was going to be very helpful to her, once she did her job for him.

But that was later, and this was now. She closed her eyes, let her head fall back, and continued to glide up and down on his hard cock. When she looked down at him again she could see he was entranced by her, looking up at her and biting his lip. He wasn't going to last very long, at this pace, but that was okay. She knew she had him, and all she needed for herself was a few more minutes.

She increased her pace, and was jumping up and down on him, now, coming down hard and coaxing loud grunts from him. She felt him tense up, and knew he was about to finish, but she didn't want him to empty out inside of her, so she hopped off just as he shot a geyser into the air, crying out as he did. He soiled the sheets and his own belly, while she managed to avoid the gusher.

She laid down next to him, one hand on his naked thigh.

"My God," he said, "that was—"

"I better go," she said, sitting up abruptly and getting off the bed. She grabbed her gunbelt from the bed post, put it over her shoulder.

"You can stay the night, if you like," he said. "And I mean . . . in another room."

"Where will I be meeting Miss Bernhardt?" she asked.

"I got her a room in your hotel."

"Then I should be there," she said. "I'll go and get dressed and let myself out."

He pushed up onto an elbow as she made her way to the door. She turned there to face him.

"Thank you for a wonderful night," she said, even though it had just been all right.

"I'll see you tomorrow, at your hotel."

"I hope . . ." she said, then trailed off.

"Yes?"

". . . that you won't feel too much guilt after I leave," she finished. "I mean . . . about your wife."

"Even if I do," he said, "it's not your fault."

She kind of thought it was, but didn't argue with him. Maybe she had misread the signs, and this had been a case of her seducing him, rather than giving in to him.

"Roxy," he said, "I—"

"I better get going," she said, cutting him off. "My driver's coming back for me."

"All right," he said, and then she was off down the hall to get her clothes. She was outside when Ted came back with his cab.

"How was your night?" he asked, dropping down and helping her into the back.

"The food was good," she said.

Chapter Eleven

There were times that Roxy didn't like the way she used men. But then she thought back to the way men used her. Even her foster father and brother had molested her along the way to her becoming Lady Gunsmith. Other men had taken advantage. Remembering all those skunks made her regrets go away.

After all, Robert Pinkerton was using her to solve a problem that he hadn't been able to solve using men. And she had no way of knowing if he would keep his word about finding her father. But she would keep hers, now that she had given it. The only man she'd ever known who hadn't misused her, or tried to, was Clint Adams, and he had recommended her for this task. That alone was a good enough reason to go through with it.

Back in her room, she thought also of another reason. She was going to get to meet Sarah Bernhardt. She had never seen the famous actress on stage, but had heard about her. She'd heard that she was a strong woman who got her way. Well, that was the kind of woman Roxy wanted to be, so meeting Miss Bernhardt could only help her with that.

She went to bed, thinking about Robert Pinkerton. She was wishing that he had lasted just a little bit longer. Instead of leaving her satisfied, she was frustrated. Somewhere along the way, in this assignment, she'd have to find a man who could take care of her, sexually.

***

She woke in the morning hungry. She'd been on the trail a long time, following up the Oregon rumor about her father, eating and drinking trail food and coffee. And she had no idea what kind of food she'd be eating on the Barbary Coast, so she decided to eat well while she was still in Portsmouth Square.

The hotel dining room was large and noisy. She knew she would be noticed when she walked in, but once she was seated, she thought she would be able to have a quiet meal with no interruptions. The two meals she'd eaten with Pinkerton had been fine, but she'd had to talk to him the whole time. She wanted a meal or two all to herself before she became somebody other than Roxy Doyle.

That was another thing. She needed some time to think of a name, and a personality. Who was she going to be while working at the Blue Lady Saloon? She certainly couldn't walk in there as Roxy Doyle.

So she suffered the attentions of the other diners as she was shown to her table, then lingered over a long breakfast, trying to carve out the new person she was about to become.

She could be anybody she wanted.

Aside from the obvious dangers, this might actually end up being fun.

***

Over a leisurely breakfast of bacon-and-eggs, a basket of biscuits and a pot of coffee, Roxy decided that she was going to be: Lulu. And Lulu was going to have a harder edge than Roxy did. She was going to have to act like she'd worked in places like the Barbary Coast, before. That meant she'd have to name some of them. And they'd have to be places that could not be checked. She would come up with a few names before she went in for the job.

Once she had decided on a name she ate the rest of her breakfast, looking around at the other diners. She wondered if Sarah Bernhardt was in the room, then decided she was not. Why would she want to be seen here if she was doing a favor for Allan Pinkerton? Roxy wondered just how close Miss Bernhardt's friendship with Pinkerton was?

"More coffee, Miss?" the waiter asked.

She looked up, saw him staring at her the way men did. He was in his forties, portly and balding. Not what she needed, at all.

"No, thank you," she said. "I'll just finish the coffee and biscuits."

"Yes, Ma'am."

He took her plate, but left the basket with a biscuit in it, her cup, and the pot of coffee. In fact, he filled her cup again before walking away.

"Thank you," she said.

"Any time, Ma'am."

After he was gone she broke apart the last biscuit, slathered it with butter, and ate it slowly. She enjoyed sitting there in the dining room, alone. Of course, she spent a lot of time on the trail alone, but this was different. Here she was surrounded by people, but was still alone. It felt . . . safe, and good.

She hadn't felt safe in a very long time, and that wasn't going to change once she started working at what Robert Pinkerton called "the Shanghai Saloon."

Her safest time had been spent with Clint Adams, learning how to handle her gun, and herself. For months, after they parted ways, she rode alone. Growing into the name the newspapers had given her. It was only three months after her training with the Gunsmith that she had first come to San Francisco, chasing a rumor about her father.

Not quite five years ago . . .

Chapter Twelve

San Francisco,
4 years, 9 months ago . . .

She rode into San Francisco on a broken down mare that needed to be put down. It had only just lasted to carry her this far. Only, she couldn't do it, herself. She had killed men, before meeting Clint Adams, and after, but she couldn't bring herself to kill the horse.

She'd heard a rumor that Gavin Doyle was in San Francisco. That he had brought in two outlaws and turned them over to the law, there, and collected his bounty. If that was true, then someone connected with the law, or the bank, would know. And they might even know where he was going when he left.

But first she had to get herself settled. Board the horse, find someone to put it down, see about a new one, and get a hotel room. The only rub was having the money to buy a new horse. Without that she would be stuck in San Francisco for a while, and would need to find a job. Unless she could find the money another way . . .

She didn't know where the bank or the police station were. In fact, she didn't know which bank would pay the bounties. She was simply going to have to keep trying police stations until she found the right one.

She needed a small hotel that would not stretch the balance of her poke. If she found a cheap enough place—both hotel and livery—she could last three days before she needed to look for work.

San Francisco was easily the biggest place she had ever been. So she had to just keep riding until she found an area she thought she could afford. She didn't know what the areas were called, but much of the city was obviously too expensive for her.

She rode for a couple of hours after arriving before she thought she was on a street she could afford. A small, two-story hotel called The Stratford beckoned to her. It had shutters on the windows that were hanging crookedly, and a roof that looked like it was in need of repair. Just right, she thought.

She tied her horse in front and went inside, carrying her saddlebags, bedroll and rifle.

"Do you have a room available?" she asked the bored looking clerk.

He wasn't looking at her when he started to answer. "Do we look like the Ritz—" he stated, but then stopped when he saw her. "Well, now . . ." He leaned his elbows on the rickety front desk. "What's a gal like you doin' in a place like this?"

"I just got to San Francisco," she said. "I'm lookin' for a place I can afford."

"Well then, you came to the right place," he said, with a nasty grin. "This is just the place for you. Room's a dollar a night."

At that rate she would be able to last more than three days.

"Good," she said, ignoring the looks he was giving her. "Can I sign in?"

"Sure."

She hoped her rep as Lady Gunsmith had not reached San Francisco, yet. She signed her real name, turned the book back to him.

"Roxy," he said. "That's kinda nice." He was in his forties, with a v-shaped face—wide forehead, pointy chin. He had a thin, cruel mouth, so his smile was somewhat less than comforting, or welcoming.

"A key?" she asked.

He reached behind him without looking away from her, plucked a key off the wall.

"There ya go," he said, looking at it briefly. "Room Seven, upstairs."

"Thank you."

She took hold of the key, but he didn't release it.

"If you need anythin', ya just gotta ask. I'm Kyle."

She tugged harder on the key, pulling it from his grasp.

"Thank you," she said. "I'm sure I'll be fine."

"Ya think?" he asked. "You're kinda young to be in a big city by yourself."

"I'll manage," she said.

She took her gear off the desk and went to the stairs. By the time she got to her floor she felt dirtier from him looking at her than she had from riding the trail.

She walked down the hall, found the door to room 7 wide open. Inside, the bed was made, but only just. She closed the door and locked it behind her, then put her gear down and sat on the end of the bed. The mattress was thick, the bed springs noisy.

Tired from the ride, she wanted to lie back and just sleep, but she still had to take care of her horse, and get herself a meal.

There was a pitcher-and-basin on the dresser, with just enough water in it to wet her hands and face. She would have to ask Kyle for more.

She forced herself to her feet and out the door.

Chapter Thirteen

In the lobby she reluctantly asked Kyle for more water in her room.

"I'll take care of it," he promised. "Anythin' else?"

"Where's the nearest place I can put my horse?"

"At the end of the street is a livery that might still be standing tomorrow."

"Sounds like one I can afford," she said. "Thanks."

She went outside, untied her horse and started to walk along the street until she reached the livery Kyle had told her about. She saw what he meant. It was small, and leaning to one side, looking like a good wind would blow it down. If she wasn't planning to have her horse put down, she wouldn't have gone in.

Inside she saw a tall, skinny man shoeing a horse.

"Help ya?" he asked, without looking up.

"My horse is done in," she said. "I think she needs to be put down, and I need to buy another one."

He dropped the horse's foot he was working on, straightened up to look at her and the horse.

"I board horses," he said, "I don't put 'em down, and I don't sell 'em."

"Fine," she said.

He was in his fifties, with grey hair and beard stubble. For a change, he was a man who wasn't looking at her with lust in his eyes. Apparently, she wasn't affecting him that way, which was fine with her.

"Can I leave him here until I find a vet?"

"Sure," he said. She handed him the reins. He looked the animal over, critically. "You've ridden her hard."

"I'm afraid so."

"I hope when you get a new horse you treat it better," he commented.

"Where can I find a vet?" she asked.

"There are a few around here," he said. "Look for a shingle."

"Yeah, thanks." She turned to leave.

"Hey!" he said. "Two bits, up front."

She dug it out of her jeans and handed it to him.

"How long do you want the animal here?" he asked.

"Until I can get it taken care of."

"Put down, you mean."

"Yeah put down."

"You ain't a animal lover, are ya?" he asked.

"No," she said, "I'm not. They get me where I want to go."

"You know the way out," he said, walking away with her horse.

***

Between the livery and the hotel she found a small café

with a menu in the window. One look told her she could handle the price, so she went inside, got a table away from the window, and ordered a roasted chicken.

"To drink?" the middle-aged waitress asked.

"Just coffee."

"I'll bring some water, too."

"Thanks."

The waitress brought the coffee and a glass of water, poured the coffee into a cup for her.

"Chicken will be right up," she said. "You look done in."

"I am," Roxy said. "Just rode in."

"Alone?"

"Yup."

"Meetin' somebody?"

"No. But I'm looking for somebody."

"Oh? Who?"

Roxy decided not to say her father, so she said, "A vet, for my horse."

"Oh, we got one who eats in here," she said. "His office is a few streets over."

"That's great," Roxy said. "Can you direct me?"

"I'll write down his name and address and give it to you before you leave."

"Thank you."

A few minutes later the waitress came back with her meal, put down a plate with half of a roasted chicken surrounded by vegetables.

"Looks good," she said.

"It is," the woman said. "We don't look like much, but we have good food. Oh, biscuits! I'll be right back."

The woman was right. The café was small, filled with mismatched tables and chairs, the paint on the wall peeling, the floor scuffed, but the food was delicious.

"Biscuits," the waitress said, putting a basket down, "and the vet's name and address." She handed Roxy a piece of paper.

"Thank you."

"No problem," the woman said, and was called to another table.

***

After her meal, Roxy paid her bill and thanked the waitress again for her help.

"Sure," the woman said, "come back again."

"I'm in the Stratford, down the street," Roxy said, "so I will."

As she started to leave the older woman grabbed her left arm.

"You wear that gun like you know how to use it, so you can probably take care of yourself," she said, "but be careful walking around this area."

"I will," Roxy said. "Thanks."

Chapter Fourteen

The vet's shingle read: George Wilkins, Veterinarian Medicine. She knocked on the door. When there was no answer she decided to look around the back. There was a long, narrow alley next to the building. She followed it back, came out into a clearing where a man was leaning over a pig.

"Dr. Wilkins?" she asked.

The man looked up at her, straightened, standing to his full height of about six-foot-two. He was a handsome man in his late 30's.

"Can I help you?"

"My horse," she said. "I just rode in, and she's done in. I think she needs to be put down."

"That's too bad. Where is the animal?"

"At a small livery at the end of the street."

"I know the one," he said. "I can go and have a look, when I'm finished here. Where can I find you?"

"I'm staying at the Stratford," she said. "My name's Roxy Doyle."

He stepped toward her, said, "I'm George," reached out his soiled hand to shake, then pulled it back. "Sorry."

"That's okay," she said. "I'll talk to you after you examine my horse."

"Fine."

She turned to leave.

"Are you here alone?"

She turned back.

"In San Francisco, I mean. You're traveling alone?"

"Yes," she said. "I travel everywhere alone."

"But you're so . . . young."

She smiled.

"I'm older than I look."

He studied her for a moment, then said, "I guess it's the gun."

"Yes," she said, "probably."

"I'll probably see you later, or tomorrow," he said. "I have to finish with this pig."

"There's no rush."

She turned and went back up the alley to the street. With the horse taken care of, and her belly full, she could turn her attention to her father.

***

She found the nearest police station. It was the only thing she thought she could do. Start with one, and keep trying until she found the right one.

She had no experience with police. Sheriffs and Marshals, yes, but she had never come across a police department. It would be something new to her.

She found the police station nearest to her hotel, after walking a good ten streets. The building was old, a two-story wooden structure that had been modified to contain the police station. It looked as rundown as the rest of the area did.

As she entered the building she saw a large front desk with a man behind it wearing a uniform. He didn't offer to help her, just stared at her expectantly when she reached him. He was in his 50's, and she saw nothing in his eyes that told her he was influenced by her beauty. He was the second man she had run into that day who reacted that way, and she liked it. Maybe in a big city like San Francisco, there were so many beautiful women men didn't act the way they did elsewhere.

"I need to talk to someone," she said.

"About what?"

"About collecting a bounty."

"You brought somebody in? Alive or dead?"

"No," she said, "I didn't bring anybody in. I want to find out if someone was brought in."

"So you're lookin' for somebody with a bounty on their head?"

"No," she said, "I'm looking for a bounty hunter."

He stared at her. "I'm not sure what to do about this. Usually a man's in here trying to collect a bounty."

"Well," she said, "can I talk to whoever it is I would see if I was trying to collect?"

"Bounties ain't paid by us," he said. "We're the police department."

"Then who pays them?" she asked.

"That'd be the sheriff."

"San Francisco still has a sheriff?" she asked.

"Oh yeah," the policeman said. "He ain't got as much to do since we came into bein', but he's still here."

This was good news. She wouldn't have to go from police station to police station.

"Can you tell me where I can find him?"

"You'd have to go to the county jail on Portrero Avenue to find him."

"And what's his name?"

"I don't—" he started, then turned his head and yelled to someone, "What's the sheriff's name?" Somebody shouted something back and he looked at Roxy again. "His name's Sheriff McKeon."

"Thanks," she said.

"Uh-huh."

He went back to whatever he had been doing at his desk, and she walked out.

Chapter Fifteen

If she was expecting to find a sheriff's office she was sorely mistaken. The building before her was huge, with a sign announcing HOUSE OF CORRECTIONS.

When she got to the front door she had to tell an armed guard what she wanted.

"The sheriff's a pretty busy man," the young guard said to her. He spoke softly while he looked her up and down with great appreciation.

"Please," she said, putting her hand on his arm. "I'll only take a minute or two."

"Well . . ." he said, softening even more. "Let me see what he says. Just wait here."

"Thank you so much, sir," she said, batting her eyes at him. Men were so stupid.

She waited several minutes and when the guard came back he was smiling.

"I can take you up," he said. "The sheriff will give you a few minutes."

"You're both so nice," she said sweetly.

She followed him down a long hall, up some stairs and down another hall, before reaching an office.

"Sheriff, this is . . . the girl who wanted to talk to you." The guard just realized he never asked her name.

"Roxy Doyle," she said.

"This is Sheriff McKeon," the guard told her.

"All right, Lawrence," Sheriff McKeon said. "That's all."

"Yessir."

The guard withdrew into the hall, closing the door behind him.

The sheriff was an older man, with white hair and a white, well-cared for mustache.

"Please, sit," he said, seating himself behind his desk. "What can I do for you?"

"I wasn't expecting to find you in a building this size," she admitted.

"It's a glorified jailhouse," he said. "Since they opened the new police department they had to find somethin' for me to do. I'm not quite ready to be put out to pasture, so . . ." he spread his arms.

"Since this is the jail," she said, "Are you the one who pays out bounties?"

"No," he said, "bounties are brought in here, I sign off on them, and then the bounty hunter gets his money from the bank. That's the way it's been done for a while." He gave her a critical look. "You're a little young to be a bounty hunter, although that gun does look like it belongs on your hip."

"Well, I—"

"Wait a minute!" McKeon said. "I think I'm gettin' it. Are you the one the newspapers are callin' Lady Gunsmith?"

"I'm afraid so."

"And you're huntin' bounty?"

"No," she said, "I'm not doin' that. But my father is, and I heard that he'd been here with a bounty recently."

"Your father?" McKeon frowned. "Who's your father?"

She had a feeling the man had figured it out, but she said, "Gavin Doyle."

"Doyle!" He spat the name like it was dirty.

"Do you know him?"

"I know 'im," McKeon said. "And you're his daughter. Well, the apple don't fall far from the tree, does it?"

"What's that mean?"

"It means you both got reputations," McKeon said. "He teach you how to use a gun, did he? When you were a kid?"

"Actually, no," she said. "He left when I was a kid. I don't really know him that well. That's why I'm looking for him"

"Take my advice," he said. "Forget it. You don't wanna know 'im."

"Well," she said, "I didn't really come here for advice, Sheriff. I just want to know if you've seen my father recently?"

"He ain't been in here with a bounty," McKeon said. "Fact is, the word I been hearin' is that he's dead, and I say good riddance."

Roxy stood up quickly, but controlled her temper.

"Then I guess I'll just get out of your hair."

"You do that, little lady," McKeon said. "In fact, why don't you get outta San Francisco. We don't need no Doyles here."

"So you say," she said, "but this is a real pretty city. I'm thinking maybe I'll have a look at it while I'm here."

"If that gun your wearin' gets you into trouble, I'll likely be seein' you back here before long—as an inmate."

"I think I can take care of myself, Sheriff," she assured him. "So don't be keeping a cell open for me."

"I got plenty of cells, Missy," McKeon said. "That's what this burg has given me to take care of."

"Well, then," she said, walking to the door, "maybe it is time for you to be thinking about retiring, Sheriff."

Chapter Sixteen

When Roxy left the sheriff's office she found the guard, Lawrence, waiting for her.

"He's not a very nice man," she said.

"He's sort of bitter about what his job has become," Lawrence said. "Come on, I'll walk you back out."

"Thank you."

She followed him down the halls and stairs to the front door, again.

"Did you just get to town?" he asked, when they were outside.

"Yes," she said, "today, in fact."

"Maybe you'd like somebody to show you around?" he asked, hopefully.

She studied him for a moment. He wasn't bad looking, and seemed fit enough.

"I'm at the Stratford Hotel," she said. "Come and see me."

"Roxy Doyle, right?"

"That's right."

"I'm Lawrence Winmore," he said. "Folks just call me Larry."

"I'll be seeing you, Larry."

She could feel him watching her as she strode away.

***

Roxy was exhausted.

On the one hand, she was happy she didn't have to go to each police station to see if her father had been there with a prisoner. On the other hand, she was deflated to find that her father had not been to San Francisco, recently.

She went back to her hotel, ignored the clerk behind the desk and went up the stairs to her room. A quick check of the pitcher-and-basin showed her that the clerk had, indeed, given her fresh water. She removed her shirt and washed her hands, face, arms and chest, then dried off with the very thin towel. Rather than don the same shirt, she took a clean one from her saddlebags—the only other one she had—and set it aside on a chair. She kicked off her boots and sat on the bed in her jeans and camisole, with her gunbelt within easy reach on the bed-post. Before long she laid on her back, and fell asleep.

***

When she woke she looked around, took a moment to get her bearings. She got up and walked to the window, and saw that it was actually dusk, but since her window was faced an alley, it seemed darker.

There was a knock on her door at that moment. She went back to the bed for the gun, slid it from the holster and carried it to the door with her.

"Who is it?'

"Larry," came a man's voice.

She frowned.

"The guard from the House of Corrections," he said, clarifying his identity.

She opened the door only a crack, still with the gun in her hand. He looked to be alone.

"Hi," he said, with a smile. "I thought I'd take you up on your offer. You know, to come and see you?"

"Oh," she said, "well, I'm not dressed—"

"I just finished work and I'm kinda hungry. I was wonderin' if you were, too?"

"Actually, yes, I am," she said. "Why don't you wait for me in the lobby. I'll only be a few minutes?"

"Okay," he said, happily. He must have been afraid she might turn him away.

She smiled at him, and closed the door.

Using the pitcher-and-basin again, to wash the sleep from her eyes. She then put on her clean shirt, and strapped on her gunbelt.

When she got to the lobby it had literally only been minutes.

He was seated in a rickety lobby chair, and jumped to his feet when he saw her.

"I'm sorry," she said, "I don't have any better clothes than these."

"You look great," he said. "Look at me, just jeans and a shirt. Don't worry about it. Come on, I'll take you to a favorite place of mine."

He walked her outside, where they stopped for just a moment.

"You wear that gun everywhere you go?" he asked.

"Everywhere." She wondered if Larry had spoken with the sheriff after she left. Did he know who she was? What she was doing there? "Is that a problem?"

"Hell, no," he said. "It'll just make me feel safe. You like steak?"

"I love steak."

"I'm gonna take you for the best steak in San Francisco. And you know what? It ain't at Delmonico's."

Chapter Seventeen

He walked her out of the rundown area of the city she was staying in, but not to an overly posh one, either.

"This ain't Portsmouth Square or Nob Hill," he told her. "But the food's gonna be real good."

While they walked he talked, telling her that he had been a guard at the House of Corrections since it opened the year before.

"I was a deputy before that, but sort of lost my job the way the sheriff did, to the new police department."

"Why didn't you join the police department?" she asked.

"Oh, I tried," he said. "They wouldn't take me. You know what they said? I was too old to be retrained. Hell, at twenty-five they said I was too old. Ain't that somethin'?"

"It's silly," she said.

"Here we go," he said. "No big windows, and no shiny signs, but really good food."

He held a wooden door open for her, and then stepped inside. She felt hardwood floors beneath her feet, saw the many wooden tables and chairs across the room. The place looked like it might have been a saloon at one time, but it didn't have the beer, whiskey, male sweat odors.

"Come on," he said, "there's a table back there."

She wouldn't have minded sitting in front, as there were no large windows, but she followed him across the floor. As they reached the table a middle-aged waiter came rushing up.

"Larry," he said, "it's been a while." He pumped the young guard's hand. "And you brought a lovely friend."

"Sammy, this is Roxy. We met today."

"Very happy to meet you," Sammy said, pumping her hand. "Larry's a nice boy, when you get to know him."

"I wanted her to have the best steak in town, Sammy. Can we do two?"

"You got it, Larry," Sammy said. "Have a seat I bring some nice lemonade—unless you want coffee?"

Larry looked at Roxy.

"Lemonade is fine," she said.

"You heard the lady, Sammy."

"Comin' up."

As the waiter rushed away Roxy asked, "Where's he from? He has a slight accent."

"Don't tell him that," Larry said. "He thinks he's gotten rid of it. Sammy came over here from Italy. If we weren't having steak we'd be having one of his Italian dishes."

"That might be interesting," she said, "next time."

Larry seemed happy with the idea that there might be a next time.

***

The steak was the best Roxy had ever had in her young life, accompanied by carrots, potatoes and onions, washed down by fresh made lemonade.

"Wow," she said, "you weren't kidding."

"Great, right?"

"More than great."

"Wait til you try desert."

"Desert?" she said. "I couldn't. I'm too full."

"Then let's share a piece of pie," he offered. "Whataya say?"

"Well . . ."

"They do a combination peach and blueberry pie that you won't believe," he said. "The berries color all the peaches blue."

"I guess that sounds like I have to try it."

Larry waved Sammy over and said, "Two coffees, Sammy, and one piece of the blueberry/peach pie."

"And two forks?" the waiter asked.

"Two forks," Larry said.

***

After the pie Roxy sat back and waved her hands in front of her.

"That's it, I'm done!"

Larry drank the last of his coffee and smiled.

"I'm glad you liked it all," he said, taking out some money.

"Oh, here—" Roxy said, starting to reach for her meager funds.

"No, no," he said, "I invited you. This is my treat."

"Let me give you some—"

"Stop," he said. "I never get to eat with a beautiful girl—not one as beautiful as you, anyway."

She stopped offering money. "Thank you."

"For the meal or the compliment?" he asked, leaving his cash on the table.

"Both."

"You're welcome," he said. "And thank you for agreeing to come out with me." He pushed his chair back. "Now why don't we go outside and maybe walk some of this off."

Chapter Eighteen

Larry took Roxy on a long walk, which included the very outskirts of Portsmouth Square. He told her how the square was filled with expensive hotels and casinos, where the high society, Nob Hill types went to eat, drink and gamble.

"Have you been to any of the hotels and casinos?" she asked.

"Not me," he said. "I don't have the clothes for it. You have to be really well dressed to get into places like the Alhambra and the Bella Union."

They continued walking, with Larry pointing out the smaller places.

"I've gambled there, and there," he said, pointing.

"How much have you won?" she asked.

"Nothin'," he said. "I'm a terrible gambler."

"Then why do it?"

He shrugged. "It's the only way to get better at it. You know, you could get into the big places."

"How would I do that?"

"With the right dress," he said. "You're so beautiful they'd let you in."

"And then what?" she asked, as they continued to walk. "I don't know how to gamble."

"You wouldn't have to," he said. "There'd be any number of men who would just want to be seen with you."

"Is that what you wanted today, Larry?" she asked. "To be seen with me?"

"No," he said, "I wanted a little more than that."

"Like what?"

He stopped walking and turned to face her. I wanted you to like me."

"I do like you, Larry. Very much."

"Oh yeah?" he said. "That's great. Then maybe we can do something tomorrow. It's my day off."

"Why tomorrow?" she asked. "Tonight's not over, yet."

"What would you like to do tonight?" he asked.

"I think if you'd come to my room in a couple of hours," she said, "I could show you."

"I-I can do that," he said, stammering slightly.

"Then I'll see you later."

"Don't you want me to walk you back to your hotel?"

"I know the way," she said. "I'll see you later, Larry."

"It'll be late," he told her. "Very late."

"Not too late," she assured him.

***

She went back to her hotel, found the same clerk behind the desk.

"I'd like a bath," she said.

"Of course, Ma'am," he said. "A bath in the morning."

"No," she said, "I want it now."

"This late?"

"I need to be clean to get a good night's sleep," she told him. "Is it a problem?"

"Ah, probably not," he said. "We got two bathtubs in the back. I'll fill one up for you."

"I'll be right down," she told him.

She went up to her room, dug through her saddlebags for some fresh underwear. The shirt she was wearing was still pretty clean, and the jeans she had on were the only ones she had.

When she got back to the lobby it was empty, but within minutes the desk clerk came out of the back carrying an empty bucket.

"The water's hot," he told her, "but it won't be for long. You better get to it."

"I will," she said, "thanks. Oh, and this," she touched the gun on her hip, "will be right where I can get to it."

He swallowed and said, "Aw, I wouldn't peek."

"See that you don't."

"Uh, it's right down that hall," he said, pointing, "on the right."

"Thank you."

She walked down the hall, found the room with the steaming tub. There was a towel on a chair next to it, and a bar of soap. She quickly undressed, hung the gunbelt on the back of the chair, and got into the tub.

The hot water closed around her as she sank down so that it was up to her neck, and she felt it enfolding her in its embrace. She closed her eyes and sat that way for a few moments, but before long she knew what the clerk had meant. The water was already beginning to chill.

She picked up the bar of soap and began to wash herself. First her arms and her shoulders, then her legs, then she sat up and began to soap her big breasts. Because she knew what she was planning for later, her nipples grew hard, so she set the soap aside and began to rub them a little harder, closing her eyes. She was starting to tingle between her legs, and knew what would happen if she touched herself there. Still, she had to be clean all over, so she grabbed the soap again, reached down between her thighs with it, and began to rub . . .

Chapter Nineteen

She got back to her room without any sign of the clerk peeking in on her in the bath. In fact, he was very careful to avert his eyes as she walked back through the lobby, her gunbelt over her shoulder.

In her room she tucked away the underwear she'd been wearing all day, then stood in front of the cracked mirror on the chest of drawers to comb her hair. She was as squeaky clean as she had been in some time, and although she had taken care of herself thoroughly with the bar of soap, she was looking forward to Larry coming by. It had been a while since she'd been with a man.

She had washed her hair, as well, and dried it rigorously with the towel, but as she ran her brush through it realized that it was still damp. She eyed herself critically in the mirror, and decided that it would have to do. Besides, she didn't think the corrections guard was going to mind. Although he had invited her to supper, and taken her for a walk, she didn't think he was very experienced with what came next between a man and a woman. She knew she was going to be able to control the situation.

She had just finished running the brush through her hair for the final time when the knock came at the door. Even though she knew it was Larry, she carried her gun to the door.

"Who is it?"

"It's Larry."

She opened the door, peered out and let him in.

"Wow," he said, "you're really serious about that gun, aren't you?"

"Did you talk to Sheriff McKeon about me after I left this morning?" she asked, holstering the gun.

"No, I didn't," he said. "I already knew all I needed to know about you."

"So you have no idea who I am."

"Roxy Doyle," he said. "What more do I need?"

He'd changed his clothes in the last two hours, combed his hair, even splashed on something that smelled like lilacs.

"Nothing," she said. "Forget it."

He looked around.

"I know," she said, "it's terrible, but it's all I could afford."

He walked to the bed, put his hand on it and pressed down.

"I only fell asleep earlier because I was so exhausted."

"You smell good," he said, "and you look great."

"Thank you."

"Are we gonna do what I think we're gonna do?"

"Well," she said, "if you think we're gonna get naked, then yes."

"Well," he said, "you might as well strap on that gun, then."

"Am I gonna need the gun in bed?"

"No," he said, "but we're goin' for another walk."

"Now?"

"I don't want to take a chance on ruinin' this experience," he said. "And that bed might ruin it. I've got a better mattress at my room. It's not a lot better, but it's got more cushion."

"Where's your place?" she asked.

"It's across town," he said. "A rooming house. We'll take a cab, be there in no time."

She studied him. Maybe he had more experience than she thought he had. He was taking charge, and she decided to let him.

"All right, then," she said, strapping on the gun, and grabbing her hat. "Lead the way."

***

They caught a cab drawn by a single horse in front of the hotel and took it to Larry's rooming house.

Larry had the cab leave them off down the street, and they walked the rest of the way.

"What was that about?" Roxy asked.

"I don't wanna wake my landlady," he said. "If she finds me with a girl in my room, she'll kick me out."

"Really?" Roxy asked. "Is it worth the risk?"

He looked at her. "You tell me."

She put her left arm through his right and smiled at him.

"That's what I thought," he said.

They went up the front steps and he pushed his key into the front door. He went in first to see if anyone was awake or around.

"There's half a dozen other boarders," he said, coming back out, "but this late at night they're all asleep."

"So I'm gonna have to sneak out early in the morning?" she asked.

"I'm afraid so," he said.

"Well," she said, "I guess I just better hope it's worth it for me."

"I guess we're both gonna find out," he said. "Come on, and let's be as quiet as we can."

Chapter Twenty

Roxy's opinion of the male sex had been formed at the hands of her foster father and brother. Since then, she had encountered few men who changed that opinion. Certainly, Clint Adams was an exception. She hadn't met many others, and it was her general intention to simply use men for her own benefit when she needed to.

What her opinion of Larry Winmore would be when this was all over remained to be seen. But at the moment, he was what she needed.

They sneaked through the house quietly, up the stairs, down a hall to his room. Once inside he closed the door gently, then turned to face her. She grabbed him and immediately kissed him. He was taken by surprise, but soon recovered and gave himself over to the kiss.

She enjoyed kissing him, so he had passed the first test. The kiss went on a bit longer, then she pulled away and looked around the room. It was small, but clean, with a real bed as opposed to what had been in her hotel room.

"I'll turn up the light," he said. There was a gas lamp on the wall by the door, and he turned it brighter, so it lit the inside of the room.

"Very nice," she said.

"Only by comparison, I'm afraid," he said. "I'm only living here because it's not expensive."

"But better than the Stratford."

"Undoubtedly."

He grabbed her, pulled her to him and kissed her. Again, the kiss went on for some time before they parted, both breathless.

"You are a tasty woman," he said.

"Thank you," she said. "You're not so bad, yourself."

"Thanks."

She walked to the bed and sat down, enjoying the way the mattress caressed her butt.

"Not bad," she said, bouncing.

He sat next to her. "Again, only by comparison."

Another pause for a kiss.

"All right," she said, pushing him away. "I think we should move on." She reached down to remove her boots. He did the same, and they tossed them aside.

At that point they stood up and both started undressing, with their backs to each other. When they turned they got their first look at each other's naked body.

"Omigod!" he said. "You're . . . amazing. I mean, I've seen naked girls before, but never anything like . . . you!"

She studied his body. He was tall and slender, but fit, no fat on him. There was no hair on his chest, but he had a heavy, dark pubic patch, and jutting from it was a very nice, semi-erect penis. It was a decent size, and still growing.

"You keep yourself in good shape," she said.

She felt him looking at her large, solid breasts, and big, rust colored nipples, so she took a deep breath.

"Oh . . ." he said.

She waited for him to approach and touch her. When he didn't, she took the bull by the horns. Or rather the horn. She walked to him and took his penis in her hand, stroked it. Quickly, it began to increase in size.

He was passing another test.

She stared into his eyes and kept stroking him. He smiled, his eyes going a little glassy.

"How's that?" she asked.

"That's . . . nice," he said.

"Remember," she said, reaching down with her other hand to fondle his testicles, "we have to keep quiet."

"Right," he said, tightly.

He finally put his hands on her with almost reverence, running his fingertips over her smooth flesh, her hardening nipples, cradling the heavy undersides of her breasts in his palms.

"Get on the bed," she said.

"Yes, Ma'am."

He went to the bed, pulled all the covers off, and did as she said. She got on from the bottom and crawled up to join him. They fell into a tight embrace, skin-against-skin, mouths fused once again, hands busy.

He was running his palms all over her, while she was more concentrated, giving her attention to his hard cock. It appeared to be as hard as it would ever get, and he definitely got a passing grade, there. She was going to make good use of it to both excite and relax herself after so long on the trail.

But first she wanted to get a real good look at it, so she began to kiss her way down his body. He moaned as her mouth moved over his smooth skin. She preferred her men not be so hairless, but when she got to his crotch that problem was solved. She used her left hand to play with his bush, her right hand to tickle his balls, while she ran her mouth and tongue up and down the length of him. His moans got loud for a moment, but then he managed to bite down on his bottom lip.

The last thing they wanted was for his landlord to discover them now!

Chapter Twenty-One

One thing she did like was the length of him. And also the smoothness of his skin there didn't bother her. She preferred that to a bumpy, veiny thing.

Finally, she moved one hand to hold his penis at the base, and took the length of him into her mouth. He groaned into his pillow, muffling the sound as she started to suck him. She smiled to herself as it became increasingly more difficult for him to keep silent. She slowed down and let his pole slide in and out of her mouth in long, easy strokes. This seemed to drive him even crazier. She felt his legs stiffen and had to stop before he finished too soon. She still had other plans.

She let his cock slide from her mouth, crawled up on top and kissed him while lying flat on him, his hard penis trapped between them.

He slid his hands down her back to cup her glorious butt, and she sucked his tongue into her mouth and sucked on it a bit before breaking the kiss.

Next, she sat up on him and looked down at his blissful face. An old whore had once told her that, in bed, men thought all women were whores, so don't ever be afraid to act like one, as long as you were getting what you wanted.

Well, what she wanted now was him inside of her, so she lifted her hips, reached down, took hold of him and rubbed the spongy head of his cock up and down her wet pussy lips.

Finally, she pushed it into her, moved her hips to take him completely inside.

She sat up straight, making sure he was firmly inside, and then started riding him up and down. This was the position she thought of as normal—this and the man on top. But she didn't like men on top of her. It reminded her of her foster father. There were other positions, of course, but she hadn't tried them, yet. She had done some new things with Clint Adams, but that had been special. She didn't mind the times Clint was on top of her, not at all.

But she had Larry right where she wanted him, beneath her, where she could just bounce on him, seeking her own pleasure and not worried about his. Of course, this evening was going to mean a lot more to him than it was to her. But one thing at a time. She would have her way tonight, and deal with the fallout tomorrow.

"Shhh," she said, as he started to groan, "we have to keep quiet, remember?"

"I don't think I can," he complained. "Jesus, this feels too . . . good."

"Stop talking," she said, with her eyes closed. She wanted to give herself up to the sensations of his cock gliding in and out of her. If he would stop talking she could do that.

She began to grunt as her time drew nearer, and as the spasms overtook her she jumped off of him and waited for the trembling to stop.

"Jesus!" he said. "Are you done?"

"I am," she said. "You're not?"

She crouched over him again and took him into her mouth. She sucked, bobbing her head up and down at increasing speed, and when she knew he was about to explode she let him slip from her mouth. As he groaned and his eyes widened she watched as his penis jumped and jerked and then, just before he ejaculated, she grabbed his shirt and held it over him so the white liquid would not spill onto him and the bed sheets.

When his cock finished pulsing she tossed the shirt aside, then laid down on her back next to him.

"My God . . ." he said, breathlessly. "Was that . . . okay?"

That was the word for it, she thought. "Okay." And she would be relaxed now that she'd had sex, but she wouldn't be going back to Larry for more.

"It was fine, Larry," she said, running her hand over his flat belly. "Just fine."

"I could go again," he said, propping himself up on one elbow and looking at her. "Just give me a few minutes to—"

"I don't think so, Larry," she said, cutting him off. "I've had a long day. I'm going to take a nap, and then sneak out of the house."

"Will I see you again, Roxy?" he asked.

"That'll depend on how long I stay in San Francisco," she said.

"And how long do you intend to stay?" he asked.

"Time enough to buy a new horse," she said. "I have to earn enough money to afford it."

"I can help you choose one."

She patted his belly and said, "Let's talk about it tomorrow, Larry."

"All right." He laid down on his back. "Tomorrow."

In moments, he was fast asleep.

***

She slept for a few hours, woke to find Larry still sleeping soundly next to her. She could tell from his breathing.

Slipping from the bed she quickly dressed, and strapped on her gun. She had to get out of the house without being seen, so she wouldn't have to try to explain anything. Peering out the door she found the hall deserted, and quickly worked her way to the staircase. They creaked as she went down. She hadn't noticed that on the way up.

She had almost made her way across the living room when a voice asked, "Who are you?"

She turned. Her eyes were used to the dark, and she could make out a little girl in a nightgown sitting on the sofa.

"Hello," she said.

"Who are you?" the little girl asked again. Roxy figured her for about 8 years old.

"I'm nobody," she said. "I'm just passing through."

The little girl frowned at her. "Whose room were you in?"

"What's your name?" Roxy asked.

"Annette."

"Well, Annette, what are you doing down here at this hour?"

"Sometimes I can't sleep, so I come down and sit."

"Are you supposed to be down here?"

"No," she said, "I usually go back up before anyone sees me. You won't tell, will you?"

So that was what was worrying her. Not who Roxy was, but if Roxy was going to tell."

"I won't tell I saw you," Roxy said, "if you don't tell you saw me. How's that?"

Annette thought for a moment, then nodded. "All right, it's a deal."

"Good-night, Annette."

"But . . . what's your name?"

"I don't have a name," Roxy said. "Remember? I was never here."

The little girl was still thinking that over as Roxy slid out the front door.

Chapter Twenty-Two

Roxy went back to her hotel and slept on her thin mattress. She'd had a fitful nap in Larry's bed because she didn't like sleeping with other people. The hotel bed was lumpy and flat, but at least she was alone, so she slept well until the room grew lighter.

First light did not stream in the room, not with the window overlooking the alley. She laid there for a few moments, replaying yesterday's activities in her head. With no sign of her father in San Francisco there was no reason for her to stay, except for the horse. She wondered if the vet might come and tell her the animal was fine, just needed some rest.

Now the vet, he was older than the young guard, Larry, better looking and probably more experienced. But he would probably think of Roxy as too young. Little did he know, her experiences far belied her years.

She got up, finally, used the remainder of the water in the basin to wash up. She could still smell Larry on her, though, so she washed again, more vigorously, using the soap she had taken from her bath.

She then went down to the street and found the café where she'd had her first meal. The middle-aged waitress remembered her and welcomed her with a big smile. For some reason, Roxy had always found herself to be able to get along well with waitresses, whether they were young, middle-aged, or elderly.

"How was your first day in San Francisco?" the woman asked.

"Not what I expected," was all Roxy would say, and the woman took the hint and didn't ask anymore.

Roxy ate breakfast, then left the café and walked to the vet, George Wilkins', office. This time she found the front door unlocked, and entered.

The outer office was empty, but she heard voices from another room. Assuming the man was busy, so she decided to wait, and sat down.

It took about ten minutes, but eventually a door opened and the vet came out, accompanied by a plain looking woman and a cute little girl, who was carrying a goat. Wilkins was wearing a white shirt with the sleeves rolled up, and was drying his hands on a towel.

"Don't worry, Caroline," Wilkins said, "your goat is going to be just fine."

"Thank you, Doctor," the little girl said. She saw Roxy. "My goat's name is Geraldine," she said to her.

"What a lovely name," Roxy said.

The little girl's mother gave Roxy a stern look, and hurried her child out the front door.

"It's a male goat, but she won't change the name," Wilkins said. "You're here about your horse."

"That's right."

"Well, I examined her and while I don't think she needs to be put down, she certainly does need to be put out to pasture. If you try to ride her, you'll ride her to death."

"That's what I was afraid of," Roxy said. "I don't have any money, Doctor. Do you know anyplace that will take her?"

"Yes," he said, "there's a farm outside of town that has a lot of land. They accept animals like your horse, who need a place to live out their days. I can take care of that for you, if you like."

"I'd appreciate that."

"And I guess we don't need to discuss my bill, if you have no money."

"Oh, I didn't mean—I have some. I can pay you . . . something."

"Never mind," Wilkins said. "It didn't take very much of my time."

"Maybe you can help me with one more thing," Roxy said.

"What's that?"

"Obviously, I need a new horse."

"But you have no money."

"Not much."

"Well, this same farm I was talking about might have a horse they can let you have. They take some animals from me that need a place to mend. There might be a horse or two out there."

"Can I walk there?"

"I can give you directions, but you can't walk it," he said. "I tell you what. I need to go out there to look in on a couple of animals. I'm going to take a horse and buggy. You're welcome to come along, if you like."

"That would be great," she said. "I'd sure appreciate it. When will you be leaving?"

"I have two more patients to look at this morning . . . can you come back in an hour or so? I should be ready to go by then."

"That's fine," she said. "I can be here." She stood up. "Thank you, Doctor."

"If we're going to spend the afternoon together," he said, "you might as well just call me George."

"Thank you, George." She extended her hand and he shook it. "I'm Roxy."

"I'll see you in an hour or so, Roxy."

"I'll be here, Doc—George," she said, and left.

The man was a hard read for her. She couldn't tell whether or not he was impressed—or even affected—by her appearance. And she found, in this case, that she wanted him to be.

Chapter Twenty-Three

Roxy spent the hour just walking around, because there wasn't much else for her to do. She was no longer looking for her father in San Francisco, she didn't want to see Larry again that day, and if George Wilkins was going to help her get a horse, then she wouldn't need to get a job to make some money. She'd just be able to leave San Francisco—hopefully.

When Roxy returned to George Wilkins' office there was a horse and buggy right out front. As she approached, the front door opened and he stepped out, wearing a black jacket, and hat.

"Ah, there you are," he said. "I'm just getting ready to leave."

"You didn't forget me, did you?"

He looked at her and said, "I'd hardly be able to forget you, now would I?" That was her first indication that he'd noticed her.

"Climb on up and let's get going," he said.

He got into the seat of the buggy from his side, then reached down to help her up from her side. Then he picked up the reins and snapped them at the horse.

***

During the ride Wilkins told Roxy something about the people who owned the farm.

"They're real animal lovers," he said. "They started by taking in an injured horse, and little-by-little began taking in other animals until they had quite a collection. It used to be a working farm, now they spend most of their time taking care of the animals."

"How do they make any money?"

"Donations started coming in from people with injured animals," Wilkins said. "Then, again little-by-little, other citizens of San Francisco began to send donations. Now, they get enough to keep the place going."

"That's amazing" Roxy said. "I can't wait to meet them."

"They're a family," he said. "Husband, wife, two grown sons, and a daughter who's just about grown. They all work out there."

"They must be wonderful people."

"They have the same family problems most people have," he said, "but they manage to make it all work."

"Sounds like a very interesting family," Roxy commented.

"What about your family?" he asked.

She looked away. "Not so interesting."

***

When they reached the farm Doc Wilkins drove the buggy right up to the main house. There were other buildings, a barn, a corral. The vet told her that it used to be a working farm. But it was probably more ranch than anything, now.

Wilkins stepped down from the buggy seat, walked around and helped Roxy down, then looked around.

"They must be out in the field, somewhere."

"We'll have to find them to talk about a horse, right?" she asked.

"Well," he said, "there should be a few horses in the barn. Why don't we go and have a look until somebody from the family comes back?"

"Suits me," she said, "as long as they don't mind."

"Nobody will mind," he said. "I pretty much have the run of the place."

"All right, then," she said. "I'll let you lead the way."

He smiled. "Follow me."

He led her to the barn connected with the corral. There were no horses outside, so they went inside.

"There," he said, pointing to two horses in stalls. "I've worked on both of those."

"Well, I'll take a look," Roxy said.

They approached the two stalls, and immediately saw the bodies.

"Oh my God!" Wilkins shouted.

Roxy moved closer, saw that both the man and woman had been shot.

"Do you know them?" she asked.

"That's—they're Dave and Amelia Hardy. They run this place."

"They were shot pretty recently," she said. "The killers may still be around."

"Oh God," Wilkins said, "their kids—Lou, Sam and Eileen. "Where are they?"

"Could they be in town?" she asked.

"No," Wilkins said, "their buckboard is still here."

"Okay," Roxy said, "maybe they're in the house."

"We should go look!" Wilkins said, and started for the door.

"Wait!"

He stopped, turned and looked at her.

"If the killers are still here, they could be in the house right now."

"But why?" Wilkins asked. "Why would anyone do this?"

"You said they get lots of donations," she answered. "Maybe the killers came for the money."

"There's no money," Wilkins said. "They get just enough to scrape by."

"Maybe that's why they're dead," Roxy said. "The killers didn't believe them about there being no money."

"So . . . what do we do?"

"They must've left their horses somewhere," she said. "If we can find them we'll know how many there are."

"And if there are no horses?"

"Then they're probably gone," she said, "and we can look in the house for the kids."

"They're not kids, really," he said. "The boys are in their twenties, and Eileen is fourteen."

"Do you have a gun?" she asked.

"No," he said, "what would I be doing with a gun?"

"Then you better stay here," she said. "I'll have a look around and see if I can find the horses."

"Shouldn't we go for the law?" he asked.

"By the time we get back to San Francisco and convince them to come out here, the killers could be gone. If the kids are still alive, they could be dead by then."

"But . . . what can you do?" he asked. "You're . . . a girl."

"Doc," she said, "I'm a girl with a gun."

Chapter Twenty-Four

Roxy left the barn, immediately went around behind it. There she found three horses tied to a hitching post. That meant there were probably still three killers in the area. One of the horses still had a rifle in the boot. She took it and went back around to the front doors of the barn.

"There are three horses in the back," she told Wilkins. "Here."

He took the rifle, but said, "What am I supposed to do with this?"

"Just . . . protect yourself."

"Wait—" he started, but she was out the front door.

Since they had left their buggy right in front of the house, it was likely that the killers knew they were there. She didn't think she could make her way to the house unseen, but that was the only way to go.

She covered the ground between the barn and the house carefully, ready to be shot at. When she reached the buggy she still hadn't seen anyone.

As she turned toward the house the front door suddenly was ripped open and two men rushed out, guns in their hands. She moved quickly as they started to shoot at her.

Throwing herself to one side she rolled and came up on one knee with her gun in her hand. She fired twice, hitting each man in the chest. They both fell over, their guns hitting the wooden floor of the porch.

She stood up, looked around for the third man.

"What the hell—" she heard behind her. She turned, pointed her gun at George Wilkins. "Wait!"

"I told you to stay in the barn!"

"I heard the shots. Did you . . . kill those men?"

"Two of them," she said. "There's probably one left, inside."

"The kids—"

"Are probably in there, too," she said. If they aren't dead already, she thought to herself.

"What do we do?" he asked.

"Stay out here," she said. "If a man comes out, shoot."

"But I can't—"

"If you don't shoot him, he'll shoot you," she insisted.

"Where are you going?"

"Around back," she said. "He'll be waiting for me to come in the front."

"Roxy—"

Again, she left him standing with his mouth open. Hurriedly, he hid himself behind the buggy and watched the front door.

***

Roxy got to the back of the house, saw that there was a rear door. She peered in the window, saw a girl lying on the floor of a kitchen. There was blood. She could tell the girl was dead. She held little hope for the two boys in the family. They were probably all dead.

She tried the door, found it unlocked and went in. Crouching next to the young girl, she confirmed that she was dead. Poor Eileen Hardy.

She went to the kitchen doorway, looked out into a dining room. The house had two stories, and she could hear someone moving around upstairs. Gun in hand, she moved to the stairs and started up. They creaked, but whoever was upstairs was making enough noise to cover it up. When she got to the top she was able to follow the sounds to one of the bedrooms.

"Goddamnit!" a man cursed. "That money's gotta be here somewhere."

She moved into the doorway, saw a man tearing the bedclothes from the bed, looking under the mattress.

"There's no money," she said.

He turned, his hand going for his gun, but when he saw her he stopped. Like the men she'd killed, he was in his 30's, dressed in trail clothes.

"What the hell—where are Travis and Ken?"

"Dead," she said.

"You killed them?"

"I did," she said. "Now, you and me are going downstairs—"

Abruptly, the man turned and ran toward the window. Before she could react, he threw himself through the glass, shattering it.

She ran to the window, saw there was a low roof outside. He had probably rolled on it, and dropped to the ground.

Doc Wilkins!

She turned, ran from the room and down the stairs. When she got downstairs she ran for the front door. As she approached, she heard shots. Running out the door she saw Wilkins, the vet, crouching behind the buggy, and the man who had jumped out the window off to the side, pointing a gun at him.

"Hold it!" she yelled.

The gunman turned toward her, and she fired, just once, but it was enough. The shot hit him, spun him around and dumped him on the ground.

She ran down the steps to the vet, who was still crouching behind the buggy.

"I couldn't," he said. "I—I've never shot anybody."

"It's all right, George," she said, taking the rifle from him. "It's all over."

Chapter Twenty-Five

She spent hours in a jail cell.

Luckily, the cell was in one of the new police stations, and not the House of Corrections, where she would have seen Larry the guard, and Sheriff McKeon.

She and Wilkins had found the two boys, dead in their respective rooms, also shot. Roxy then sent the vet back to San Francisco for the police, never expecting that when they arrived, they would arrest her and toss her in a cell.

She was sure that Wilkins was telling them exactly what happened. At some point they would have to come and let her out. But she understood that she had killed three men, and there was going to be an investigation. Especially since the police department was new, and wanted to justify themselves.

So she laid on her cot, and waited.

***

Eventually, she heard the sound of keys, and somebody approaching. A middle-aged man in uniform appeared and slid the key into the lock.

"Let's go," he said.

"Where?"

"They want you upstairs."

"Am I still under arrest?"

"We'll see, little lady," he said, "we'll see."

He walked her ahead of him, out of the cell block, up a flight of stairs and down a hall to a room. The walls were grey, as were the table and chairs in the center of the floor.

"Have a seat," the man said. "We'll be right in."

But they didn't come right in. She sat there for another hour before the door opened, and three uniformed men walked in. There was the middle-aged one who had brought her there, a younger man who stared at her openly, and then an older man who seemed in charge—in command, actually.

"Miss Doyle," he said, as the younger man closed the door behind them, "I'm Chief Benjamin Anderson, Chief-of-Police here."

"Am I still under arrest?" she demanded.

"You've killed three men in my jurisdiction," he said. "I take that kind of thing very personal."

"Those three men killed a whole family of innocent people," she pointed out. "Do you take that serious, too?"

"Never mind, young lady," he said. "I know who you are."

"I'm just somebody visiting your fair city," she said.

"Somebody quick with a gun."

"Look, what did you want me to—"

"Never mind trying to defend yourself," he said. "San Francisco doesn't need the likes of you, Miss Doyle."

"Did Doc Wilkins tell you what happened?" she demanded.

"We know all about it," he said. "Now look, I'm gonna let you out of here, but I want you to leave San Francisco,—right away."

"I'm happy to do that, believe me," she said. "Coming here was a waste of time."

"This is officer Bowman," he said, indicating the young man. "He'll show you out."

"What about my gun?"

"You'll get it back at the front door," the Chief said. "Bowman, take her out."

"Yessir."

Roxy stood up and walked to the door.

"And Doyle."

"Yes?"

"I don't want to see you back here," he said, "ever!"

"That suits me, Chief."

She followed the young officer through the halls to the front door. This wasn't the station she had come to looking for her father, but it looked the same, with the big front desk.

"That way out, uh, Ma'am," Bowman said. He was still staring at her with watery eyes.

"My gun?" she asked.

"Oh, yeah." He walked over to the desk, where the other man handed him her gunbelt. "Here ya go."

She took it, but didn't put it on right away.

"Thanks," she said.

"Sorry you have to leave San Francisco, Miss," he said. "Real sorry."

"Yeah, well," she said, "I'm not."

She went out the front door, paused long enough to strap on her gun, and then walked down the stairs.

"Roxy!"

She turned, saw Doc Wilkins standing by his buggy, waiting for her.

"How long have you been out here?" she asked.

"Not that long," he said. "They had me inside, too. I thought I'd wait for you, though, give you a ride."

"I appreciate that."

"Well, I appreciate what you did out there," he said. "You probably kept me from blundering in and getting killed. Come on, climb aboard."

They got up onto the buggy and Wilkins snapped his reins at the horse.

"I'm sorry about that family," she said.

"So am I," he said. "They were good people. They didn't deserve to die like that, for nothing."

"Who'll run that place now?" she asked.

"I don't know," he said. "Maybe nobody. Do you want to go to your hotel?"

"Just to check out," she said. "The Chief told me I have to leave, which suits me."

"Where are you headed?" he asked.

"I have no idea."

***

When they got to her hotel she dropped down from the seat and said, "Thanks."

"I'll wait here for you."

"You don't have to."

"How do you expect to leave town?"

"I have a little money," she said. "I might be able to get a train ticket to the next town on the line."

"I have a better idea," he said.

"What's that?"

"I'll just wait for you, and show you."

"Well . . . all right. I'll be right back."

***

When she came back out with her saddlebags and rifle he was standing by the buggy. He helped her up, and then joined her, once again snapping the reins at the horse to get it moving.

"Where are we headed?" she asked.

"My office."

"What's there?"

"You'll see."

It wasn't a long ride, and as they pulled to a stop in front of Wilkins' office, she saw a few horses tied up in front. There were other stores around him, so she thought nothing of it.

He helped her down, took her saddlebags and rifle for her, and then walked over to a horse.

"This one's for you," he said.

"What?" she asked. "But . . . where—"

"It's one of the horses that was in that barn," he said. "I figured you have it coming for what you did."

She walked over, ran her hands over it, found it to be a fit colt.

"I don't know what to say," she said.

"Don't say anything," he said. "The saddle's yours, I got it from the livery."

He handed her the saddlebags and rifle, and she put them on the saddle.

"I'm sorry you have to leave," Wilkins said. "I would have liked to have gotten to know you better."

"I was thinking the same thing."

She gave him a hug, then turned and mounted the horse.

"If you come back this way—" Wilkins said.

"The Chief told me never to come back," she said.

"But who knows?" he asked.

She looked down at him, smiled and said, "Yeah, who knows?"

PART TWO

Chapter Twenty-Six

San Francisco,
Roxy's present . . .

Replaying her first visit to San Francisco in her mind reminded Roxy of the Chief-of-Police's warning that she shouldn't come back—ever! She wondered if the police situation was still the same, and if Benjamin Anderson was still the Chief. Maybe Robert Pinkerton knew . . .

After breakfast, she went back to her room to await Pinkerton's arrival. He was going to have to put her together with Sarah Berhardt for lessons on how to play the part of a saloon girl. She'd seen saloon girls before, but according to Pinkerton, the Blue Lady Saloon had a better class of girls than the other Barbary Coast establishments. Better girls, better dresses.

She was only there for half an hour when there was a knock at the door. Answering her door was still something she never did without a gun in her hand. Originally it was on the advice—no, the orders—of Clint Adams, but now it was based on her own experiences. Several times in her life someone had simply fired a gun through the door, trying to kill her.

She stood to one side and said, "Yes?"

"Robert Pinkerton, Roxy," the voice said.

She cracked the door and allowed him in.

"Are you ready?" he asked.

"For what, exactly?" she asked.

"To meet Sarah," he said. "I'm going to take you to her room."

"Right now?"

"Let's go."

He was smiling, which was a good thing. She was wondering if it was going to be awkward between them, if he knew that it hadn't gone very well between them in bed, and she had just used him for some momentary satisfaction. Thankfully, none of that was evident.

"Lead the way," she said.

He opened the door, looked both ways in the hall—just normal caution—and stepped into the hall ahead of her. She went out, closed her door, and followed him.

"I hope you understand," he said, as they walked, "but we put her in a suite."

"That's fine with me," Roxy said. "She deserves it."

They stopped in front of a door.

"She's not registered under her own name, and won't be seen on the street very much. She really doesn't want anyone to know she's here."

"I understand. But what do I call her?"

"She's registered as Marie Delorme."

"Where'd that name come from?"

"It's a Victor Hugo play," he explained, "that didn't go very well for her."

Pinkerton turned and knocked.

Roxy had seen photos and tintypes of the actress over the years, but did not know what she really looked like. Every image was different, because she was playing a different part. So, when the door opened she had no idea what to expect.

What she saw was a young woman smaller than her, almost slight. She had honey-colored hair and a pleasant, pretty, perfectly made-up face. Roxy knew that she was in her mid to late 30's, but at that moment she looked a lot younger. Then she realized that if Miss Bernhardt wanted to do this without being recognized, this was probably what she didn't really look like, either.

"Miss Delorme," Pinkerton said, "meet Miss Doyle."

"It's a pleasure," Sarah Bernhardt said in perfect, English, even though Roxy knew she was French-born. "Come in, please."

Pinkerton allowed Roxy to precede him into the room, but did not close the door behind them.

"I'll be back sometime later this afternoon," he said. "By then we should all be hungry."

"You're not staying?" Roxy asked.

"No," he said, "you two ladies don't need me. You both know what needs to be done. Miss Doyle, Miss Delorme."

"We will see you later, Robert," Sarah/Miss Delorme said.

Roxy decided she was going to have to start thinking of her as "Miss Delorme," until someone told her different.

Pinkerton left, closing the door behind him.

"Can I offer you something?" Miss Delorme asked. "I had them bring up hot tea, coffee, and some brandy."

"What are you having?" Roxy asked.

"Tea, just now."

"Then I'll have tea, too."

"Excellent."

The suite had two rooms. The one they were in was furnished with an overstuffed sofa and armchairs, heavy brocade drapes covering the windows, a desk in one corner with a chair, and a round wooden table with four chairs. On the round table was the tray holding the tea pot, coffee pot, brandy decanter, cups, saucers, and glasses.

As Miss Delorme walked to the table to pour the tea Roxy asked, "Um, are we allowed to talk freely here?"

The other woman turned and smiled at her.

"Of course," she said. "We in this room know who I am. And you may call me Sarah. Shall I call you Roxy? Or Lady Gunsmith?"

"Roxy will do."

"There," Sarah said, handing Roxy a cup filled with tea. "we've managed to dispense with the unnecessary annoyances of false names. Sugar?"

"No, thank you."

"Let's sit and talk," Sarah said, "and we'll be able to figure out what to do with you. Although, I must say, you are stunningly beautiful."

"Thank you," Roxy said, blushing.

They sat at the table, across from each other.

"I'm quite serious," the actress said. "I don't think I've ever been on the stage with a woman as beautiful as you—and furthermore, I don't want to." Roxy frowned. "No one would give me a second look." Sarah made the last statement with a smile.

"If I can ask," Roxy said, "how do you know the Pinkertons?"

"I met Allan first, many years ago when he was in England working on a case. It was before he came to America and started his agency. I was a very young girl and he made use of my acting talents, even then."

"I see."

"We remained friends," she said. "I wrote to tell him I was coming to America to tour, and when I arrived there was a telegram waiting for me. And, here I am."

"Well, I appreciate that you're here," Roxy said.

"Why don't we talk a little about what you'll be doing," Sarah suggested. "Then we can work on your character."

Chapter Twenty-Seven

Roxy and Sarah drank the tea, and then switched to the brandy. Eventually, they moved into the other room of the suite, the bedroom. There was a dressing table with a large mirror, which Sarah sat Roxy at. They spent a lot of time there, going through different kinds of what some people called "face paint," but Sarah referred to as make-up.

At times Roxy was dismayed, thinking she looked like a clown. At one point she said, "All I'm missing is the big red nose!" But Sarah patiently talked her down, reminding her of the girls she'd already seen in saloons and dancehalls.

"Besides," Sarah added, "with the low décolletage you'll be sporting, none of them will be looking at your beautiful face, the fools."

"Low?" Roxy said, touching her chest.

"Very low," Sarah said. "A lot of skin is expected in these places."

"You've been to these places?"

"Not in San Francisco," she said, "but many just like them in London—mainly in places like Liverpool. You look surprised."

"I just didn't think that you . . ."

"I performed in many suspect establishments in my early career, Roxy," Sarah said. "You have to work your way to the top, you know."

"I suppose you're right."

What Sarah did with Roxy's red hair was simply pile it atop her head, showing her how to keep it in place with just a few pins.

"Usually," Roxy said, "when I do that it's to stuff it underneath my hat."

"Well, now we're going to want people to see it," Sarah said. "But as I told you, even with your glorious hair and beautiful face, people—men—will be looking at that bountiful bosom of yours—which, by the way, I wish I had."

"I've seen photos of you on stage, Sarah," Roxy said. "You're very beautiful."

"You see?" Sarah said, with a smile. "The magic of make-up. Not that you need very much magic, my dear."

Roxy was starting to become uncomfortable with Sarah's constant compliments. Was the actress simply trying to boost her confidence? Roxy Doyle really didn't need a booster, she knew she could take a man down with her beauty or her gun, almost any time she wanted to.

She'd heard stories about Sarah Bernhardt and her many lovers. But she'd never heard anything about Sarah Bernhardt and other women.

"I am sorry," Sarah said, suddenly. "I seem to be making you uncomfortable."

"No, it's not—I mean, I'm used to women giving me . . . disapproving looks. I don't usually get compliments from ladies . . . unless . . ."

". . . unless they are interested in you?" Sarah asked, laughing. "Oh, my dear, I get those kinds of offers all the time.

Most women are either going to want to be you, or see you fall. It's envy and jealousy."

"Aren't they the same thing?"

"Not at all," Sarah said. "Someone can envy you without wishing you ill. But jealousy . . . that's a different story. If another woman is jealous of what you have, or how you look, she'll want to see you tumble. There, I think your hair is perfect this way."

Roxy looked in the mirror. Most of her flaming red hair was piled atop her head, except a few artful tendrils that hung down here and there.

"That's . . . beautiful."

"Yes, it is," Sarah said. "Now let's get your face done so Robert can get the whole effect when he arrives. "And my dear—" she touched Roxy on the arm, "—make sure he gives you plenty of money for the gowns you'll need."

***

When the loud knock came at the door they were still busy in the bedroom. Sarah was putting the finishing touches to Roxy's face.

"Wait here," Sarah said, "and only come out when I call you."

"All right."

As Sarah Berhardt left the room, Roxy once again beheld herself in the mirror. The hair, the make-up, even the stature the actress had lectured her on, were all so alien to her. And yet she liked how she looked. She had gotten used to seeing

119

Lady Gunsmith, a legend, and not a flesh and blood woman in her mirror. This was a revelation to her.

Sarah had worked miracles.

She was still looking in the mirror, turning her head to the right and left, when she heard Sarah call her name. She stood up, took one last look. The only thing that ruined the effect were the clothes she was wearing. Sarah had gowns in the closet, but they were much too small for Roxy, who was taller and bustier than the famous actress.

Well, there was no way to fix that, so she just squared her shoulders, turned, and walked into the other room.

Chapter Twenty-Eight

Robert Pinkerton stared in stunned silence.

"Well?" Sarah asked.

"Amazing," he said. "You're stunning, Roxy."

"Thank you."

"I mean . . . truly stunning," he went on. "And normally you're . . . you're lovely, but this . . . I'm speechless . . ."

"Do you think she'll get hired?" Sarah asked.

"I think she'll definitely get hired," Robert Pinkerton said. "No question."

"If that's true," Roxy said, "I'm going to need the right clothes."

"Why do I think this is going to cost the agency a lot of money?" Pinkerton asked.

"Well, I'm going to need the right gowns for this Shanghai Saloon," she said.

"When you get there," he warned, "don't call it that. Remember the proper name."

"The Blue Lady."

"That's it."

"I'm still going to need the right dresses," she pointed out.

"Let's talk about that over lunch, shall we?"

***

Pinkerton left the hotel with the two ladies—Roxy still had her hair up, but Sarah was wearing a black wig, trying to avoid being recognized.

Pinkerton wanted to take them to an expensive restaurant, but Sarah insisted on something a little less ostentatious. She thought there was more chance of being recognized by a member of San Francisco's upper crust. So, instead of a place on Nob Hill, he decided to go halfway and took them to a Market Street restaurant.

"Have you been to the Blue Lady?" Roxy asked Pinkerton, when they were eating.

"No," Pinkerton said, "I have to admit I've not been there myself. I'm going to send one of our local operatives with you as far as the front door, just to be safe."

"Well then," Roxy said, "I'll have to go and apply for the job before I shop for dresses. They may want me to dress a certain way."

"Oh, I am certain of that," Sarah said. Pinkerton looked at her. "I've not been to your Barbary Coast, but it sounds a lot like Liverpool. I think the men there will appreciate a daringly low décolletage, don't you?"

Pinkerton looked at Roxy. "Is that going to be a problem?"

"Well," she said, "it's not what I usually wear, but it sounds as if this job will call for it."

"What about," Sarah asked, looking at Roxy's hip, "that? You certainly can't wear that around your waist when you're wearing a brightly colored and revealing gown."

"It'll be revealing on the top," Roxy pointed out, "not on the bottom, right?"

"Well," Sarah said, "some men might want to see some leg."

"Then," she said, "I'll have a gun in a holster strapped to my thigh—under my dress."

"And if somebody gets handsy and feels it?" Pinkerton asked.

"Hey," Roxy said, "I'm a girl working in a dangerous place."

"That'll work," Pinkerton said.

They had managed to get a back table, where Roxy wouldn't be near a window, and Sarah wouldn't be on display. But at that moment a man and woman seated a few tables away were looking at them, and talking excitedly.

"Uh-oh," Pinkerton said.

"I see them," Roxy said.

"Who? What's wrong?" Sarah asked, looking up from her chicken.

"It looks like one of you might have been recognized," Pinkerton said.

"In this country," Sarah asked, "wouldn't it be more likely to be one of you?"

"Not me," Robert said. "There's no reason for anybody to recognize me."

"I guess that leaves you, Roxy," Sarah said. "I understand you have a certain reputation."

"I do," Roxy said, "in some places, but I didn't think it would be here."

"Well," Pinkerton said, observing the obviously excited couple, "they recognize somebody."

"Perhaps we should move along before they decide which one of us it is," Sarah suggested.

They were all pretty much finished with their meals, so they agreed, and stood up to leave . . .

***

They almost made it, but when they got outside the couple came rushing out and approached them.

"Excuse us," the man said, "but aren't you Sarah Bernhardt?"

"I'm sorry—"

"We saw you on stage in London," the woman said. "You were brilliant."

"I don't think—"

"We were amazed to see you—"

"Excuse me," Pinkerton said, "but you're obviously mistaken."

The man looked at Pinkerton and frowned.

"No, we ain't," he said. "We saw her on stage, wearing a black wig just like this one."

"Oh, it's her," the woman insisted. "Why would you insist it's not?"

"Because it isn't," Roxy said.

"Well," the woman said, lifting her nose as she stared at Roxy, "I admit, I was wondering why she would be sitting with someone as trashy as you, but—"

"Okay, that's enough!" Pinkerton snapped. "Move on before I call the law."

The man and woman looked shocked, took a few steps back, and then as Pinkerton ushered the two ladies away, started to squabble between themselves.

"See?" the man said. "I told you it wasn't her!"

"It was too!" the woman insisted.

"I'm sorry about that," Pinkerton said to Roxy and Sarah. "They had no right—"

"But that was marvelous!" Sarah insisted.

"What?" Pinkerton asked.

"Didn't you hear the woman say how trashy Roxy looks?" Sarah asked.

"Oh, yeah . . ." Roxy said, getting it.

"I'm sorry . . ." Pinkerton said, helplessly.

"Robert," Sarah said, "we got her look just right!"

Chapter Twenty-Nine

Sarah went back to her room, refusing to go shopping with Roxy. She didn't want to take a chance on being recognized—again.

"Besides," she added, "you said you were going to apply for the job first."

"That's true," Roxy said.

In the suite, however, Pinkerton took out some money and passed it over to Roxy.

"Just so you can go shopping right after you get the job."

"You're still sure I'll get hired?"

"Oh yes," Pinkerton said, "especially after the work Sarah has done with you."

Roxy looked at Sarah. "How much longer will you be in town?"

"I'm catching an afternoon train tomorrow."

"Good," Roxy said, "I should have time to show you the dresses I buy."

"Definitely."

"Then I guess I'm off to the Shang—the Blue Lady Saloon," she told them. "Wish me luck."

"You won't need it," Sarah said. "They'd be foolish not to hire you."

"Uh," Pinkerton said, "you're not going to wear your gunbelt when you apply, are you?"

"I'll figure something out," Roxy said. "I may be playing a saloon girl, but that doesn't mean I'm going to go unarmed."

***

The Blue Lady Saloon was more Barbary Coast than most of the saloons were. In fact, it was located on the docks. When sailors got off their ships, it was easy to make the Blue Lady their first stop for drinking, gambling, and women.

Pinkerton assigned a man named Sam Warren to accompany Roxy to the front door. He was a small, nervous looking man, a local who did small jobs for the Pinkertons.

"I hearda you," he said to Roxy. "Don't know why the Pinks think you need me to keep ya safe."

"I think they just wanted to make sure I got to the right place," she said, with a smile.

"Well," Warren said, "there ya go." He pointed to the docks. "Right down there. And be careful. The docks ain't no place for a lady."

"That's okay, then," Roxy said. "I'm not supposed to be a lady."

It was early, but that didn't keep the place from being busy. Above the front door was a portrait of a woman, her face tinted blue. As Roxy entered, still dressed in her trail clothes, men turned and looked at her, watched her walk to the bar. Some of the saloon girls turned to look, as well. When she reached the bar, several men made room for her.

"Well, hello, darlin'," one said. "Can I buy you a drink?"

"Maybe some other time," she said. "I'm here on business."

"What kind of business, sugar?" another man asked.

"The kind I need to talk to the bartender about."

"Hey, Wood!" one of the man shouted. "Got a pretty lady here needs to talk to ya."

Roxy had hoped she wouldn't run into any trouble. Her gun and holster were hanging on the bedpost in her room. All she had on her was a small 2-shot derringer tucked into her cleavage, inside her buttoned shirt. She didn't want anybody to see it, and getting to it quick would be a problem.

"I'm busy," Woodbury, the bartender said, when he came over. "Whataya want?" He was a rough looking character, black, in his early 40's, stern but not bad looking.

Roxy crooked a finger at him so that he leaned over the bar to hear what she had to say.

"I'm lookn' for a job," she said.

"What kinda job?"

"The kind you hire women to do in a place like this," she said. "What else?"

Woodbury straightened up, looked her up and down and rubbed a hand over his jaw.

"Well," he said, "yer good lookin' enough."

"Thanks."

"But you'd have to talk to the boss."

"And who's the boss?"

"Rex Burns," Wood said. "See that door all the way in the back, next to the stage?"

"Yes."

"Go knock on the door and tell him I sent you," Wood said. "He'll interview you."

"Thanks."

"Listen, he might ask you to do some, uh, weird things, but once you get the job it'll be worth it."

"Weird how?" she asked.

"You'll see. Just don't be too shy when you go into his office."

"What's your full name?" she asked.

"I'm Woodbury Jefferson."

"Well, Woodbury," she said, "once I get the job you'll find out I'm not the shy type."

"By the way," Wood asked, "you wouldn't be carryin' a gun, wouldya?"

She decided not to lie.

"As a matter of fact, I am."

He looked her up and down.

"Where?" he asked.

"Tucked in where you won't get to see it," she told him.

Woodbury smiled, showing even, white teeth.

"The boss is gonna like you," he said. "Go on, go talk to 'im."

"Thanks, again."

She turned, left the bar and headed across the room, attracting attention as she went. But most everyone there had seen her talking to Woodbury, so no one got in her way.

Chapter Thirty

She knocked on the office door.

"Yeah?"

She opened the door and stuck her head in. A handsome man in his late 30's was seated behind a large, wooden desk that took up most of the small room.

"Mr. Burns? Rex Burns?"

"That's right," he said. "What can I do for you?"

"Woodbury sent me to talk to you," she said, "about a job."

"Is he recommending you for the job?"

"No, sir," she said, "I'm applying. He said I had to talk to you."

"Well, come on in," he said, "and let me take a look at you."

She stepped into the office, closing the door behind her, and turned to face him.

"Come closer, girl," he said. "I'm not gonna bite you."

She took a few steps, stopped a foot or two from the desk.

"Well," he said, standing up, "you're good-looking enough, that's for sure."

"Thank you."

He walked around the desk and stood in front of her. They were almost eye-to-eye.

"And you're tall."

She didn't comment.

"You got red hair . . . all over?" he asked.

She wondered if this was where it got weird. Was he going to ask her to undress? And if he did, should she?

"Yes, sir," she said, "All over."

"That's good. You got the freckles?"

"I do," she said, "A lot of 'em."

"You redheads and your freckles," he said. "Turn around once for me."

She made a complete turn, came back around to look him in the eyes again.

"Can you sing? Dance?"

"No."

"Ah," he said, "the way you look, it ain't gonna matter. You got dresses?"

"Some," she said, "but I didn't know what you'd want me to wear."

"We're gonna want to see those freckles," he said. "That means shoulders and bosom bare."

"Uh, how bare?"

"You mind takin' off your shirt?"

She hesitated, then said, "No, I guess not."

She unbuttoned her shirt while he watched, then peeled it off, held it in her left hand.

"About that bare," he said, "no more. Wow, you are beautiful, aren't you?"

Again, she didn't comment.

"What's that?" he pointed to her cleavage, where the butt of the derringer was just visible.

"This?" she asked, taking the gun out.

"What's that for?"

"Protection."

"If you're workin' here, you won't need it," he said. "We'll protect you. In fact, Woodbury's the bouncer."

"He looks pretty tough," she said.

"He is," Burns said. "Spent a lot of years in the ring. You can put your shirt back on."

She tucked the derringer away, and donned her shirt, buttoning it.

"You got a room?"

"In a fleabag hotel."

"Good," he said, "we'll give you a room upstairs. You can leave the gun there."

"I can do that."

"Take today to buy some dresses, if you need them," he said, going back around his desk and seating himself. "What's your name?"

"Rachel Dolan!" That was the name she and Sarah had come up with. It was Irish, and had the same initials as her own, so she was more likely not to forget it, which would be embarrassing.

"Well, Miss Dolan, welcome aboard," he said.

"Uh, what will I be doing?"

"When you come back with your dresses and whatever other belonging you have we'll put you in a room upstairs," he said. "At that point, you'll talk to Doreen Henderson. She runs the girls. She'll tell you what you have to do, and what you can do if you decide to do it. Okay?"

"Okay. What about my pay?"

"Whatever you can pick up, and a portion of the drinks you sell," Burns said. "A lot of the girls make more than twenty-five dollars a day. And that's without the sex. You can talk to Doreen about that. Okay?"

"Sounds okay," she said.

"One more questions," he said.

"What is it?"

"Why here? Why my place? Why not someplace in Portsmouth Square. I mean, a woman who looks like you . . ."

She made a face and said, "I don't like those people. Upper crust? From Nob Hill and areas like that? Not for me. I thought the people down here on the coast would be real."

"Oh, they'll be real, all right," Burns said.

Chapter Thirty-One

Roxy went back to her hotel. She had to check in with Pinkerton, tell him she got the job, and then talk to Sarah about where to buy the dresses. Sarah wouldn't go shopping with her, but could certainly guide her to the right stores.

Pinkerton wasn't around, so she knocked on Sarah's door and gave her the news.

"That's wonderful!" she said, then added, "I think. This will be dangerous, won't it?"

"It might be," Roxy said, "but I'm committed, and I've already made contact."

"Did they like you?"

"Oh, yes," Roxy said. "The bartender and the owner, both."

"Well then, you're on your way," Sarah said. "The Pinkertons will be very happy."

"I really appreciate your help, Sarah. Now if you'll just give me an idea of what stores to go buy my dresses from."

They discussed it for a short time, and then the two women hugged.

"I won't see you again before I go to my train tomorrow," Sarah said. "I wish you luck."

"You're going back on your tour?"

"Yes."

"Then I wish you luck, too," Roxy said, "not that you'll need it."

"One always needs luck," Sarah said. "No matter how good one is."

***

Roxy went out and did her shopping. When she returned she spread the three dresses she'd bought out on the bed, and there was a knock at the door. Gun in hand, she answered it and let Pinkerton in. He had something wrapped in brown paper under his arm.

"I assume from this wardrobe that you got the job," he said.

"I got it," she said. "I'm supposed to go over there either tonight or tomorrow and get a room. Also to talk to the head girl."

"She's going to explain that whether or not you have sex for money will be up to you," Pinkerton told her. "I want you to know I don't expect you to do that. It's not part of the job."

"Listen," Roxy said, "about what we did—"

"That's not important," he said, cutting her off. "From here on it's business. Okay?"

"Okay."

"Do you want to go back over there tonight, or tomorrow afternoon?"

"I might as well go tonight and get situated," Roxy said.

"All right, then," he said, "I'll leave you to pack. What about this?" He pointed to her gunbelt, hanging on the bedpost

"I'm taking it," she said. "I'll wrap it in one of the dresses, and hide it in my room. I'll just feel better having it near."

"Well then, you might want this." He held the brown paper package out to her.

"A gift?"

"You could call it that."

She tore it open and found it to be a leather holster, but unlike any she'd ever seen before.

"It goes around your thigh," he said. "You'll have to get used to walking with it, but I think you'll manage."

Roxy walked to the bedpost, took her gun and slid it into the thigh holster.

"A perfect fit," she said.

"I thought it might be," he said. "I noticed your gun wasn't full size. I assume that's something Clint Adams made for you?"

"It is."

"All right, then I guess you're all set," Pinkerton said.

"How do I keep in touch with you?"

"Sam," Pinkerton sad. "He's a fixture on the docks. Nobody will suspect anything if he's around. You can send me messages through him."

"Okay, good."

"The minute you have evidence that they're shanghaiing men, you let me know through Sam and I'll do the rest."

"All right."

"And don't do anything silly," he said. "All I need for you to do is get information. Not take any action on your own."

"Understood."

"Be careful, Roxy," he said, at the door. "I'm missing men on this assignment, and they might be dead. I don't want to have to wonder about you, too."

"I'll be very careful, Robert."

He went out and she started packing her dresses, wrapping both holsters. She had brown paper bags from the store, and stuffed everything into them. She also decided to take her saddlebags. It wouldn't be a secret that she had come riding into town on a horse.

She was uncertain about what to do with her rifle.

Chapter Thirty-Two

She walked into the Blue Lady with her arms full. Several men presented themselves and offered to carry her things. She managed to fend them off, and went to the bar, where Woodbury spotted her.

"Back already?" he asked. "Can't wait to get started?"

"No time like the present," she said.

"Hang on." Woodbury looked out over the sea of bodies in the saloon, saw who he wanted and started waving. A woman came walking over. She was wearing a glittery blue off-the-shoulder dress. She had long dark hair and clear smooth skin, looked to be in her early 30's.

"Doreen," he said, "this is . . ." He looked at Roxy.

"Rachel Dolan."

". . . Rachel," Woodbury said. "She's the new girl the boss told you about."

"Well," Doreen said, "the boss was right. You are a beauty."

"Thanks. You're beautiful, too. You have lovely skin."

Doreen ignored the compliment. "The boss wants me to get you settled, so you might as well follow me and I'll take you to your room."

"Lead the way."

"Need help carrying anything?"

"No, I've got it all." Roxy didn't want anyone wondering about the weight of the brown paper bags.

"Why don't I take that?" Doreen asked, indicating the rifle that was dangling from Roxy's hand.

Normally, she would have said no, but under these circumstances she had to say, "Fine."

Doreen grabbed the rife, and led Roxy across the saloon floor to a stairway that led up. On the second level, they walked along a section that overlooked the saloon floor, and then they turned into a hallway. One of the doors opened and a blonde girl came out, hanging onto a drunken guy's arm. She smiled at Doreen as they passed.

"That's Cora," Doreen said. "She does a lot of business up here."

"You mean sex?"

"Oh yeah," Doreen said. "Nobody expects you to do that unless you want to. All you have to do is serve drinks, and be nice to the customers."

"Nice?"

"You know, flirt, get them to buy drinks. The more drinks they buy, the more money you make. Got it?"

"I got it."

"You got dresses?"

"Yes."

"I'll need to see them."

"As soon as I unpack," Roxy said. She wondered how she was going to do that without Doreen seeing her gun and holsters.

"I'll give you a chance to get settled, then come back," Doreen told her.

"Okay, Roxy thought, that works.

Doreen opened a door and allowed Roxy to go in first. It was a small room with a bed, a dressing table and mirror, and not much else.

"It's kind of bare right now," Doreen said, "but it's yours. You can do whatever you want with it."

"It's okay," Roxy said, "for now."

"Get yourself settled in and I'll be back in . . . say. . . half an hour to look at your dresses. Do you want to get to work tonight?"

"Sure, why not?"

"Then you might as well pick out a dress and put it on," Doreen said. "I'll be able to judge better if I see it on you."

"I'll do that."

"Good," Doreen said. "See ya later."

After she left, Roxy quickly unwrapped the clothes, took out the gun and holsters and hid them under the bed. Then she spread the dresses out on the bed, picked one and put it on.

Chapter Thirty-Three

When there was a knock at her door half an hour later Roxy did not have time to think about answering it with her gun in hand. The door opened immediately following the knock, and Doreen walked in. First, she reviewed her dresses and pronounced them adequate for the job. "Maybe a little too fancy, but we can deal with that. At least they're long enough. Our boss likes the girls wearing longer dresses than most saloon girls, makes the customers wonder what's underneath."

Roxy stood up from the dressing table and turned to face the other woman.

"Well," Doreen said, "you certainly look presentable."

Roxy turned and looked into the mirror again. The dress showed off her shoulders, and the upper slopes of her large breasts. The freckles in her cleavage were very evident. Her hair was just the way Sarah Bernahrdt had shown her to do it.

"Just presentable?" she asked, turning back.

"Well," Doreen said, her hands on her hips, "if anythin', you look too damn good for this place."

"What should I do different?" Roxy asked.

"Lemme show you," Doreen said.

She walked up to Roxy and immediately started taking pins out of her hair. In moments, she had the long red hair resting on Roxy's shoulders.

"If anything," Doreen said, primping, "you need to use this hair like a curtain, Hide behind it, a little. See?"

Roxy turned to the mirror again, squatted down to take a look. She saw what Doreen meant, as the hair not only covered her shoulders, but would also hide her cleavage if she swung it properly.

"That's why you see a lot of saloon girls constantly playin' with their hair," Doreen explained.

Roxy had not noticed that in the past, but said, "Okay, I get it."

"Good. Oh, and the face paint," Doreen said.

"What about it?"

"Well, too much and, again, too perfect," Doreen said. "You don't wanna drive these cowboys and dock workers past what they can resist. I mean, already you're better than anything they've seen here before."

Doreen grabbed a cloth from the dressing table and began dabbing at Roxy's face.

"Nothin' drastic," she explained, "just a little touch here and there . . . okay. Take a look."

Roxy turned to the mirror yet again and saw what Doreen had done to Sarah Bernhardt's perfect make-up application. Doreen was right, it wasn't a drastic change, it was just somewhat . . . muted.

"The way you looked woulda popped if you were on stage," Doreen said. "But here you don't need to pop."

"I understand."

"There," Doreen said, "now you're ready to make your debut."

"Thank you for your help."

"No need to thank me," Doreen said. "I'm doin' my job, and if I didn't do it, I'd hear it from Burns. Come on, I'll walk you down."

They left the room together, and Roxy was glad that Doreen didn't have much to say about the dress. She didn't need the woman to start poking around beneath it and finding the holster that was strapped to her right thigh. It was somewhat awkward walking, but in reality, the gun was just a little lower than it would have been in a normal holster. The only problem was going to be pulling up the dress to get to the gun if and when she needed it.

"Stop here," Doreen said, as they reached the area looking down over the saloon. "Let's let them have a look at you this way, first."

Little-by-little the customers began to notice her, and the more of them who looked up, the more others followed.

"You wore the right dress," Doreen said. "That emerald green really goes with your hair and eyes. What else did you bring?"

"Blue and red."

"You'll have to get more green," Doreen said. "Don't ever wear the blue. If you notice, none of the girls are wearin' blue."

"Does that have something to do with the name of the place?" Roxy asked.

"Oh, yes," Doreen said. "A woman the boss was seeing when he opened this place, she always wore blue dresses."

"And what happened?" Roxy asked. "Did she die?"

"Oh, nothin' so dramatic," Doreen said. "She just . . . left."

"So, does that mean that you're his woman now?"

Doreen looked shocked at the question, and laughed.

"Oh, no," she said, "the boss doesn't have one woman now. So, you better watch your step. He'll be after you soon enough. But don't worry. Once you give in he won't bother you, anymore."

"If I give in," Roxy said.

"Right."

"Well," Roxy said, "we'll see, then."

"Yes," Doreen said, "we will."

Chapter Thirty-Four

Roxy's first week as a saloon girl was uneventful.

The men appreciated her, made comments, and grabbed at her as she went by, but no more or less than they did the other girls. Oh, there were occasions when a sailor, dock-worker, cowboy or merchant got out of line, but Woodbury certainly was able to handle those problems all by himself. And it wasn't always trouble with one of the girls. Often, it was just a drunk or a bad loser at one of the tables.

As for Rex Burns, he had not made any sort of advance towards her during that time. And neither had she seen him with any of the other girls. He seemed to be all business.

Now, whether or not that business had any connection with shanghaiing men onto ships that were leaving port, she didn't see or hear. The Blue Lady seemed to be nothing but a Barbary Coast Saloon and Gambling Hall, as advertised.

By her 8th day Roxy—or "Rachel"—had pretty much been accepted by the customers, and other saloon girls, all of whom seemed to be just slightly younger or older than she was. The only one who appeared to be over 30 was Doreen.

She took her tray to the end of the bar. When Woodbury saw her, he came over.

"Whataya need?"

"Four beers, please, Wood."

"You been here a week, girl," Woodbury said. "You don't gotta keep sayin' please."

"Sorry."

He drew four big frosty mugs of beer and set them on her tray. This had been the hard part for Roxy. Not getting the dress and make-up right, not walking with the gun strapped to her thigh, but balancing the tray when it was filled with drinks. Often, she had mugs of beer along with shots of whiskey or, in many cases, a bottle. The first few nights she'd gone to bed with both arms aching, but she was getting the hang of it, now.

She carried the tray of beers to a table of four waiting men who had arrived several minutes earlier. They all looked and smelled like they had just come off a ship. These were the types of men Doreen had warned would give her the most trouble—at least, when they first came in.

"Here you go, boys," she said, setting the beers down. "Enjoy."

"I tell you what I'd enjoy, lassie," one of the men said, in a Irish lilt. "I'd enjoy seein' you outta that pretty green dress you got on."

"Well," she said, "that would cost you a lot more money than you've got, handsome."

He wasn't handsome by any means. He was short and squat, sturdily built, with several spaces in his smile where he was missing teeth.

The other three men laughed at Roxy's comment, but the squat man seemed to take umbrage.

"Now wait just a minute, lass," he said, "how do you know how much money I've got?"

"It doesn't really matter honey," she said. "That's just not something I do. There are other girls here that'll take you upstairs, though."

As she started to walk away he reached out and grabbed her left wrist. He had big hands, with thick, calloused fingers.

"We ain't done negotiatin', lass," he said.

"We're done, friend," she told him, trying to jerk her wrist free, but his grip was like iron.

Another of the girls, a small blonde named Lily, saw what was happening and went to the bar. In the next second Wood came out from his position and crossed the room.

"We got a problem here?" he asked.

"No problem, Wood," Roxy said, "this gent was just about to let me go."

"This gal and me was negotiatin', is all," the man said. "She don't think I got enough money to take her upstairs."

"You don't," Wood said. "Nobody does. She don't go upstairs with anybody."

"Well," the man said, "maybe we can change that right now."

He kept hold of Roxy's wrist and stood up. The other three men with him shrank back a bit, either from their friend's actions, or from Woodbury's presence.

The sailor was almost half Woodbury's size, but he was younger, and obviously very strong. Roxy didn't know what the next few moments would bring, but she wasn't tempted to go for her gun. The situation did not seem to warrant her giving its presence away.

"Now friend," Wood said, "If ya wanna sit back down and let the girl go, the house'll be glad to buy your table a round of drinks."

"Hey, now, Jimmy," one of his friend said, "That sounds like a good deal."

But Jimmy stared up at Woodbury's face, then let his eyes wander over the rest of the black man's frame.

"You know, friend," he said, "I'm real curious about what would happen if you and me tussled, but . . ." He released his hold on Roxy's wrist, ". . . right now it's more important to satisfy me and my friends' thirst. So, you send over that free round of drinks, why don't you, boy?"

"It's on the way."

Jimmy sat down with his friends, while Woodbury took hold of Roxy's left elbow and guided her to the bar.

From behind the bar he started to draw the men another round and said to Roxy, "I can have one of the other girls bring these over."

"No," she said, "it's okay, I can do it. I can't run away from situations like that."

"You did good." He set the four new beers on her tray.

"How'd you know I was in trouble?" she asked. "I can't even see that table from here."

"You got Lily to thank for that," Wood said. "She saw what was goin' on and tipped me off. Ah, here she is."

Roxy turned and saw Lily approaching with a smile on her pretty face.

"You okay, Rach?" she asked.

"I'm good, Lily. Thanks for the help."

"Ah, it was nothin'," the smaller girl said. "You takin' these over there?"

"Yeah," Roxy said, "a round on the house."

"Come on, then, I'll go over with ya, help ya set them down."

"Thanks, Lil."

Chapter Thirty-Five

Lil was Lily Gardner, and turned out to be Roxy's best friend after two weeks. She had the room next to hers. Lil was one of the girls who made extra money by taking men up to her room. Very often Roxy heard sounds she could recognize coming through the walls.

At the beginning of week three on the job Lil came into Roxy's room without knocking, sat on the bed and watched her get ready for work.

"I wish I had a body like yours," she said, wistfully.

"You seem to have plenty of men wanting to go up to your room with you," Roxy said. "And you've got a pretty face and cute little body."

"Yeah, cute," Lil said, "but look at you. You're . . . luscious."

"Well, thank you kindly," Roxy said.

"I mean it, Rach," Lil said. "If you'd take men up here you could make a fortune. I'll bet they wouldn't rut and squirt and then go to sleep on you."

"Is that what happens?" Roxy asked, turning around on her seat. She was wearing a red dress that day, even though she'd bought a few extra green ones. The blue one was rolled up into a bundle.

"Well," Lil said, "they try to go to sleep, but I hustle them out so they can do it somewhere else." She shook her head. "I don't mind takin' men to my room, but I ain't about to sleep with them."

"I know what you mean," Roxy said. "I like to sleep alone, myself." She stood up, smoothed down the front of her dress. "Well, I guess we better go down."

Lil jumped up from the bed and hurried to open the door for Roxy. The little blonde was her usual bundle of energy.

As they stepped out into the hall they ran into another girl, a brunette named Kate Merchant. She was tall and lean, almost skinny, and she had her share of men who liked girls that way.

"Hey, girls," she said. "Look at us, we got it all covered. Short, tall, and voluptuous."

"Luscious," Lil said. "I just told Roxy she's luscious."

"Yeah, well," Kate said, "she's got luscious tits, that's for sure."

The three girls walked down the stairs together, under the watchful eyes of the customers. It was early in the evening, and the saloon was not teeming with men, yet, but the ones who were there were appreciative.

As Roxy hit the floor one man in particular caught her eye. She walked over to the bar to lean on the end of it, and he moseyed over and set his beer down. To anyone watching, it would look like he was just talking one of the girls up.

"How are you, Sam?" she asked Sam Warren.

"I'm fine," Sam said, in a low tone, "but it's been two weeks and Mr. Pinkerton is kinda worried."

"Tell him I'm okay, and I'm working on getting myself accepted, here."

"Well, since you been here two more men have been shanghaied. He wants to know if you have anythin' to tell him, yet?" Sam asked.

"No, nothing," she said. "If they're shanghaiing men from this saloon, I haven't seen any sign of it, yet. But I've got something to ask you."

"What's that?"

"Don't be obvious about it, but there are two men sitting underneath the painting of an old man across the room. Do you know who they are?"

Sam took his time but eventually caught a glimpse without being obvious about it.

"I don't know them, but they look like they've got money."

"That's what I was thinking," Roxy said. "I've seen them in here about three times, always sitting there, and always drinking the same thing, something called Jasper Hole Whiskey."

"I never heard of it."

"Well, see what you can find out about it, and them. Now finish your beer and get back to Pinkerton. Come in here every few days, as you have been. When I get something, I'll let you know. And you find out what you can about those two."

"Whatever you say," he replied, and directed his attention to his beer.

Roxy moved away from him, found herself confronted by the one girl in the place who didn't like her. And the feeling was mutual.

Mona Hendricks was a tall, beautiful woman with hair the color of molasses. She was full bodied, and showed herself off in such a way that men took bets on if and when her breasts would bob free from her bodice.

"What're you doin' with that runt?" she asked Roxy. "Tryin' to drum up some business?"

Roxy smiled. "I told him a nickel would get him a visit to your room."

"A nickel? Why you—"

Roxy walked away from the blustering Mona. She knew that the girls working the streets and alleys were getting a nickel a poke. She wanted Mona to know that's what she thought she was worth.

Mona apparently thought Roxy had a superior attitude, since she didn't take men to her room. It also looked to Roxy like Mona had her cap set for the boss. She was always co-zying up to him, and seemed to think that "Rachel" was her biggest competition.

"What did that bitch want?" Lil asked, coming up along-side Roxy.

"Just making a comment, like always," Roxy said.

"She doesn't like any of us, but she really hates you," Lil said.

"That must be why I hate her," Roxy said.

"What about you and the boss?" Lil asked. "Anythin' there, yet?"

"Not now," Roxy said, "and not ever."

"I guess she doesn't believe that."

"Too bad for her," Roxy said. "As far as I can see, the field is clear for her . . . if he's interested, which he's not."

"I know," Lil said, "he's not interested in any of us." She wiggled her eyebrows. "I know, I've tried."

"Can we get some beers over here?" a voice came from a table full of men.

"Comin' up!" Roxy called back. "Let's get to work, Lil."

Chapter Thirty-Six

"Rachel!"

Roxy turned. When Woodbury called like that he usually wanted her to do something. He waved her over to the bar.

"What is it?" she asked.

"I need you to go in the back and get me two bottles of Jasper Hole whiskey."

"Jackson Hole?"

"*Jasper*! It's a private brand we stock for special customers."

"Okay," she said, "Jasper Hole. Got it."

"It should be in a box stacked against the near side wall."

"Okay," she said, again.

She went through a doorway that was at the end of the bar, down a short hall and into the back room, where all kinds of liquor bottles were stored. This was the first time Woodbury had sent her back there. She decided to take advantage of that fact and have a look around.

She had been to every other part of the building, and not found anything that would indicate a shanghaiing operation was being run from there. This was the only room she hadn't been able to search yet.

First she found the Jackson Hole, took two bottles from the box and set them aside. Then she started to snoop around the room.

Perhaps there was a reason she had not been sent back here until more than three weeks after she was hired. Could it be that Woodbury was starting to trust her?

She looked around, checking the walls first, and then the floor. When she stood still she could hear water beneath her. If there was some kind of trap door, that might be the way they were taking men out.

Of course, there was a rear door that led to the back of the building. Men could certainly be carried out that way, too.

When she thought she'd taken too long she grabbed the two bottles of whiskey, and carried them out to Woodbury. He was apparently so busy he hadn't noticed how long it had taken her.

"Thanks. Now hold on." He opened one of them, poured out two glasses. "Take this over to that table underneath Zachariah."

"Zachariah" was a painting that hung on the wall. It was of an old, bearded man and none of them knew who he was, so they named him Zack. It hung right over one of the tables.

"Right."

She put the two shot glasses on her tray, along with the bottle, and carried them over to the table. There were two men sitting there who looked as if they didn't belong. They were in their 40's, and well dressed. In fact, they were expensively dressed and, oddly, no one in the place seemed to be paying attention to them. Normally, men dressed like that would be receiving measuring glances from men trying to figure out when and where to rob them.

"Here you are, gents," she said, setting the glasses down, and then the bottle. Instead of bending at the waist to put it down, she had been taught by the other girls to bend her knees.

"Only bend at the waist if you think it's gonna get you a good tip," Lil had told her. "The men will be waitin' for your tits to fall into their laps. Jeez, I wish I had tits like yours, I'd be bending over at every table."

Roxy kept that in mind, and only at certain times did she bend over. This was one of those times.

Both men's eyes were rooted to her breasts as she leaned over to set the whiskey down. She took the opportunity to look them over, and saw that both were carrying guns in shoulder rigs. She could see the bulges under their jackets.

"Thank *you*, sweet thing," one man said.

"Do those things ever fall out of that dress, honey?" the other man asked.

"Only when I want them to, handsome," she said, and flounced away, knowing they were watching her. "Flouncing" was something else little Lil had taught her. And it was something else she only used on special occasions.

Like this one.

Chapter Thirty-Seven

At the start of the fourth week Roxy was frustrated.

Yet another man had been shanghaied according to Sam Warren, and she still had nothing. So, she decided something drastic needed to be done.

That was why she woke up in Rex Burn's bed one morning, but that was after . . .

***

Burns lived on the third floor of the building. There was no access to that floor for the public. In fact, nobody could even see the stairs that led up there. You had to walk all the way to the end of the second floor hallway to get to those steps. So each morning, when Burns came down, he had to walk past all the girl's rooms.

Roxy contrived to be at her doorway when Burns came down that day. He was wearing, as usual, a black suit, and a white shirt. She was wearing a flimsy robe, and her hair was down, in sexy disarray.

"Good morning," Burns said. "How are you doin', Rachel?"

"Well, I'm not sure," she said, with her arms folded across her breasts. "Maybe we can talk about it in your office?"

"Sure," he said. "My door's always open."

"Well . . ." She dropped her hands to her sides, which allowed the robe to open slightly. Beneath it she was naked. Roxy was glad none of the other girls were in the hall to see this. ". . . maybe we should leave the door locked."

Burns smiled at her. "Why don't you come down when you're ready to talk, Rachel? I'll be having breakfast at my desk, this morning. You could join me."

"Thanks for the invitation, boss."

He looked at what he could see beneath the robe, her belly button and the slopes of her breasts, and said, "I could say the same thing,"

As he continued on down the hall Roxy hastily closed her robe and backed into her room, closing the door. She felt dirty, but this job had to get done. It was going on way too long.

She quickly got dressed, with one of her more severe dresses, which didn't show too much skin. It was the blue one. She wanted to see what effect it had on Burns.

She went downstairs, still not having run into any of the girls that morning. From Lil's room next door she'd heard a lot of commotion the night before, so she knew the little blonde would be sleeping in, to recover. She seemed to have encountered a man who didn't just squirt and go to sleep.

Woodbury was sweeping the floor. When he saw her he stopped and stared.

"Are you crazy?" he asked.

"What do you mean?"

"No blue dresses around the boss," he said. "Didn't Doreen tell you that?"

159

"But he invited me to his office for breakfast," she said. "This is all I have."

"Girl," he said, "you're gonna get yourself kicked out of there."

"I don't think so, Wood," she said. "I think he's interested."

"In you?" Wood asked. "He ain't interested in any one woman, Rachel. You're gonna find that out the hard way."

"Well," she said, "that's the way I've found out most things in my life."

"Go ahead, then," Wood said. "His breakfast was waitin on his desk when he went in, and there's plenty. That's if he don't throw it at you as soon as you walk in."

"Tell me something, Wood," she said.

"What?"

He continued sweeping.

"Who was the Blue Lady?"

"That ain't for me to tell," he said, stopping and leaning on the broom. "If he wants you to know that, girl, he'll tell you hisself."

He went back to his sweeping.

Roxy turned and walked toward Burns' office, knocked on the door.

"Come in," he called from inside.

She opened the door, entered, and stood there for his inspection. The effect of her blue dress was going to be interesting.

"Have a seat," he said, barely looking at her. He was busy with the food on his desk, which was now set up like a restaurant table. "What's your preference, eggs or flapjacks?"

"Eggs," she said.

"Coffee?"

"Of course."

When he finally looked up at her and saw her in the blue dress, to his credit, he paused only a moment, then held out her chair.

"Come and sit," he said, "and tell me what's on your mind, Rachel."

Chapter Thirty-Eight

She walked over and sat, and he pushed her chair in. The desk was covered with food, as if he had been expecting a guest. But even she hadn't known she was going to be there until that morning.

"This is a lot of food," she said, as he sat across from her. "Who were you expecting?"

"You've been here almost a month," he said. "I thought it was time. If you hadn't been standing in your doorway, I was going to knock."

"You're kidding."

"I'm not," he said, handing her a plate with eggs and ham on it. "Biscuits?"

"Yes, please."

He placed a basket of warm biscuits near enough for her to grab, then helped himself to some flapjacks.

"We haven't talked very much since you started working here," he said. "Not since the day I hired you. What's on your mind?"

"Well, to be honest, you are."

"Should I be flattered," he asked, raising his eyebrows.

"I don't know," she said. "I was warned when I started that you might . . . try something."

"Try something?"

"You know," she said. "With me. They said you tried to have your way with all the girls, at least in the beginning."

"And then what?"

"And then you were done with them."

"And who was telling you all this?"

"You know . . . some of the other girls?"

"Doreen?"

"No," she said, "not Doreen. She doesn't talk about you."

"And did 'they' say why I did this?"

"Just that it had something to do . . ."

"Yes?"

". . . with the Blue Lady."

"What else did they tell you about 'the Blue Lady?'" he asked.

"Just that I shouldn't wear any blue dresses," she said. "And that was a warning."

"But today," he said, "you are wearing a blue dress."

"Yes, I am."

"Because you wanted to get a reaction from me?"

"I suppose so."

He stuffed his mouth with flapjacks and molasses, chewed, then looked at her and asked, "How are your eggs?"

"Fine," she said. "Thank you."

"Well," he said, "suppose I tell you why I was going to knock on your door this morning?"

"All right."

"I was going to invite you to breakfast."

"And here we are."

"Yes."

"And the point of this was?"

"As you said," he told her. "To try something with you."

"Why?"

"Well first, you're beautiful," he said, "and second, I thought you'd be curious by now."

"You thought right," she said.

He smiled and said, "Precisely."

"So, you were playing with me."

"Playing," he said, "but not necessarily a game, really."

"You could make me sleep with you," she said, "by threatening to fire me."

"Did anyone tell you I ever tried that?"

"No."

"Good. I never would. Sleeping with me would have to be your own choice."

She stared across the table at him. He was good-looking, of that there was no doubt. And charming. He didn't have to force women to sleep with him. Lil was quite willing to, and would again. Mona was after him all the time. Roxy wondered if he'd slept with Mona, yet.

"If I did sleep with you, I'd have to be careful."

"Why's that?"

"Mona?"

He stopped eating and stared at her.

"What about her?"

"She'd probably kill me," Roxy said. "She's in love with you."

"She is not!"

"Well," Roxy said, "she wants to be with you."

"That's entirely different," he said, eating again. He washed down a mouth of food with some coffee. "Don't worry about Mona. She won't try anything."

"Are you sure?"

He smiled. "I'm positive."

She decided since they were talking, she might as well broach a couple of other subjects. She knew she was taking a chance on him becoming suspicious, but something had to be done to speed this process up.

"What can you tell me," she asked, "about shanghaiing?"

He stopped eating and stared.

Chapter Thirty-Nine

"Where did you hear about that?"

She shrugged. "People talk."

"Did you hear the name they have for this place?"

"You mean 'the Shanghai Saloon?'"

"That's ridiculous!" His face grew red and he looked legitimately angry. "If this place was being used to shanghai men, I'd know about it."

"Would you?"

"I know every inch of this place," he said. "All right, tonight I'd like you to come up to the third floor after you've finished working."

"Wow," Roxy said, "an invitation to the third floor?"

"And you know what's going to be expected of you," he told her.

"Oh, yes," she said, trying to seem eager.

They finished their breakfast and Burns said, "You better get to work."

"Yes, sir." She stood up. "Thank you for breakfast."

She started for the door, then stopped and turned back.

"One more question?"

"Go ahead."

"Why would anyone call this place 'the Shanghai Saloon?'"

"Jealousy," he said. "There are a couple of saloons and halls near here who are competing with us. They're not as successful, so they start rumors."

"Are there men being shanghaied, though?" she asked.

"Probably," he said. "I don't concern myself with that. It's not even against the law, but I don't approve of it. I don't want my customers waking up from a drunken stupor and finding themselves on a boat in the middle of the ocean. It's bad for business. That's why I say it's not happening here. And by the way, why are you working early? I prefer to have you out there in the evenings."

"I traded with Lil," Roxy said. "She needed some extra time this morning."

"Are you working tonight, too?"

"Yes, I'm doubling. Since I don't take men to my room, I can use the extra money."

"Well, you better get to work, then."

"Yes sir."

"And I'll see you tonight."

"Yessir!"

She left his office and went out onto the saloon floor. It was very early in the day, but the Blue Lady was always open, the liquor was always flowing, the gaming tables were always busy and the girls were always on the floor.

On this day Roxy was working the floor with a girl named Patty. She was in her late 20's, slender and pretty, with long brown hair.

"I hate workin' this early," she said, as Roxy walked over to her. "Nothin' ever happens."

Patty was one of the girls who didn't go upstairs with men. She delivered drinks, and flirted. That was it.

"You never know," Roxy said. "In a place like this, anything could happen."

And something did. Something unexpected.

The batwing doors opened about an hour later, when there were just a few men drinking, and gambling. A man walked in and approached the bar. Roxy and Patty were standing at the far end, and Roxy frowned, thinking she recognized the man. Was he one of Pinkertons? Had he been sent in to check on her instead of the nervous Sam Warren.

And then she got it, and she knew she had to get to him before he saw her and ruined everything.

Patty started to move, and Roxy put her hand on the girl's shoulder.

"He looks boring," she said. "I'll take him."

"You can have him."

Roxy left her position at the end of the bar and walked over to the man while he was ordering a drink from Woodbury. Just before she reached him he turned, as if to look the place over with a beer in his hand, and saw her coming.

"Oh, my God!" he said, as she approached. "It's Rox—"

"Rachel!" she said. "Hi, I'm Rachel."

He frowned. "Rachel?"

"Welcome to the Blue Lady," she said. "Have you ever been here before?"

"Uh, no," he said, looking puzzled. "This is my first time."

Woodbury was still within earshot, so she continued to play the part.

"And what brings you here today?" she asked, trying to put him off with her expression so he wouldn't say her real name.

"I was in the area on business," he said, "and saw the place, and thought I'd have a beer."

As Woodbury walked further down the bar Roxy lowered her voice and said, "Well, I never expected to see you here."

He lowered his voice as well and said, "And I never expected to find you in San Francisco again, let alone in a place like this. What's going on?"

"Let's go and sit," she said. "Bring your beer. I don't want anyone to hear us."

"Do you have a room we could go to?" he asked.

"I have a room, but I don't take men there," she said. "Just follow me."

She turned and walked to a table that was as far from the bar, and other people, as she could get, so they could talk without being heard.

They sat and she asked George Wilkins, "Now tell me what a vet is doing on the Barbary Coast docks?"

Chapter Forty

"There are animals on the docks. But first," he said, "tell me why Roxy Doyle is working as a saloon girl called Rachel? Is this your new career? Have you put down your gun, and your Lady Gunsmith name?"

"No," she said, almost in a whisper, "I'm still Roxy Doyle, but I can't tell you right now what I'm doing here. I just don't want you to give me away."

"Ah," he said, "so you're working on something. Are you in danger?"

"Not if you keep your mouth shut."

"Shut is the word, then," he promised. "My God, you look beautiful. I mean, you were lovely—what was it, five years ago? —but now . . ."

"Almost five," she said, "and thank you. I'm not exactly comfortable in this getup, but . . ."

"Well," Wilkins said, "if you ask me, you should wear dresses all the time. Tell me, do you have any that, uh, show more?"

"Yes." she said, "this is my daytime dress. At night I do, uh, show more."

"Well then," he said, "I'm going to have to come back tonight."

"No—wait, yeah, okay, you can come back," she said. "Just don't give me away."

"Okay," he said, leaning in, "but when whatever this is you're working on is done, we have to have supper together."

"Agreed."

He finished his beer and made to get up, but stopped when she said, "One more thing."

"What?"

"That Chief–of–Police who was here the last time? Anderson? Is he still here?"

"He is," Wilkins said, "but I don't think you'd have to deal with him down here. Why?"

"Just curious."

As Wilkins left, Roxy realized she probably wouldn't have to deal with any law, since Shanghaiing was not illegal.

Unless somebody got killed. That would definitely change the game.

***

The Blue Lady started to fill up a few hours later, and soon more girls were working the floor, and more gaming tables were busy.

Roxy forgot about Wilkins the more drinks she had to deliver, and the more hands she had to avoid. Most of the men grabbing at her were regulars, who grabbed at each of the girls as they went by. There had only been that one occasion when Woodbury had to step in and help her. All-in-all she did not find working on the Barbary Coast such an unpleasant, and dangerous experience. Then again, she didn't spend that much time outside, except for a few shopping excursions with Lil

171

and some of the other girls, and those had taken place during the day. At night, they were in the saloon, or in bed, and would hear shots from outside, but she was never curious enough to do more than go to a window and look outside. It was usually somebody letting off steam.

As she came to the end of her double shift, she thought about the invitation to the third floor to be with Rex Burns. Pinkerton had told her he didn't expect her to sleep with anyone for this job, but this was a chance to get close to the boss maybe learn something. And it was also an opportunity to satisfy her own curiosity about him. He was charming and handsome, but how was he in bed? Generous and skillful? Or boring—like most men?

Tonight, she'd find out all of that, and maybe more.

***

That night the two men in the expensive suits were there again, sitting underneath Zack. She didn't serve them this time, but kept her eye on them. Oddly, they not only didn't talk to anyone, but they hardly spoke to each other. She still found them suspicious.

After work, she went back to her room just to freshen up a little, then made her way down the hall to the stairs up to the third floor. When she got to the top there was no hall, no door, just a wide expanse of living space, with expensive, plush furniture, fancy rugs and light fixtures.

"There you are," Burns said, from the far side of the room. He was holding a drink in each hand. "Brandy?"

"Why not?"

She crossed the room toward him. He took a few steps, as well, and handed her the drink.

"What kind of day did you have?" he asked.

"Busy."

"Are you . . . too tired for this?"

She smiled and said what she thought Rachel Dolan would say. "I'm never too tired for this."

"Glad to hear it."

He was still wearing his black suit. She had changed into a green dress with an extremely revealing neckline. It looked as if all she needed to do was take a deep breath and her breasts would burst from the dress.

"Tell me something," he said.

"What?"

"Why are you really here?"

"You invited me," she said, "or don't you remember that?"

"No," he said, "I mean here, working in my saloon. You could have gotten a job anywhere in San Francisco, the way you look."

"I thought I explained that when I applied," she said, setting the glass aside on a nearby table. "Besides, I'd heard stories about you."

"Is that right?"

She knew there was only one way to get him to stop asking questions. She reached behind her, undid her dress, and allowed it to drop to the floor. When she'd gone to her room to freshen up and change her dress, she'd made sure that all she had to do was drop it, and she'd be naked.

She took a deep breath, causing her breasts to swell, and stood with her hands on her hips.

"You still want to talk?" she asked.

His mouth had obviously gone dry. He wet his lips with his tongue, put down his own glass, said, "No!" and reached for her . . .

Chapter Forty-One

Sometime later he pressed his face to her red pubic patch, and probed through it with his tongue. They were in his bedroom, on his expensive over-sized bed. She was on her back, and as he probed her she opened her legs wider, to give him better access. He certainly knew what he was doing. His tongue was touching all the right spots, causing jolts of pleasure to run through her.

"Oooh," she said, reaching down for his head.

He had grabbed her in the other room, kissed her and ran his hands all over her naked body. At the same time she'd done her best to get his clothes off of him. When his cock came into view it was long and hard and she grabbed for it. Right there and then she'd dropped to her knees and taken him into her mouth. She sucked him, wetly, avidly for what seemed like a long time, but it was only minutes. He'd grabbed her, pulled her to her feet, and practically dragged her to the bedroom, where they were now.

"Oh, yes," she said, as he used his lips along with his tongue. He sucked her pussy, and peppered it with kisses that continued to jolt her.

"Damn," she said, wrapping her hands in his hair, "get up here."

He didn't fight her, and crawled up onto her, kissing his way up her body until he was biting and sucking her big nipples, his hard, hot penis trapped between them.

"We have all night," she said, scratching his sheets, "for God's sake, fuck me."

He smiled down at her. "I always try to give a lady what she wants."

He moved his hips and she felt that spongy head of his cock press against her wet pussy lips. Then, with a quick move, he was inside of her, filling her up. He began to move, slowly at first, and then with increasing speed. She reached down and dug her nails into his muscular buttocks. He had a wonderfully fit body without any sign of fat.

She wrapped her legs around him, and finding his rhythm, matched it, moving her ass to correspond to his thrusts.

"God," he said, "you're steaming hot . . ."

"That's because of you," she said, into his ear.

She let him plow her that way, sliding his hands beneath her to palm her ass cheeks. Then, abruptly, she decided she wanted to be on top.

She knew she surprised him with her strength, as she flipped him onto his back. For a moment, his cock came out of her, but she jumped right back on it, taking it deep inside, so deep that she imagined she could feel it all the way up to her breasts, as if the head of his penis was between them.

She rode him that way until they were both covered with sweat, and then reversed her position on him. She was still riding him, but this time her back was to him. It was a different angle and it touched her in different places, plus she knew from past experience that he—like any man—would not be able to take his eyes off her ass.

He was very good in bed, but she was still the one in control . . .

***

She woke the next morning in his bed, feeling rested and spent at the same time. Burns wasn't in bed next to her, and then she realized why. He was in the other room, talking to someone, and it was a serious conversation.

She had nothing to wear, so she grabbed one of his shirts, put it on and walked to the door. She didn't go through, just stood there and listened.

". . . coming to me with this?" Burns was asking.

"We figure he was down here, he must've been a customer of yours."

"Well," Burns said, "I have lots of customers. Talk to my bartender. He pretty much sees them all."

"So, you don't recognize him by name?" a man asked. Burns seemed to be talking with two men.

"I never heard of him. Sorry."

"Okay, Mr. Burns," the other man said, "sorry to bother you this early."

"That's okay," Burns said. "I would help if I could."

She heard the sound of walking, and then someone going down the stairs. She turned and got back to the bed just in time. Burns came through the door.

"Sorry," he said, "did that wake you?"

"I just heard voices and wondered where you were," she said. "Who was it?"

"The police," he said. "Two detectives from San Francisco's new police department."

"New?"

"Well," he said, "about five years old." He sat on the bed with her, reached over and touched the collar of the shirt she was wearing. "Anyway, they had some questions."

"About what?"

"A body found on the docks last night," he said. "They're thinking he might have been a customer of mine."

"Did you know him?"

"They told me his name," he said. "I never heard of him. And I have no idea what a vet would be doing on the docks."

Her stomach went cold.

"A vet?"

"Yeah, they said he was a vet," Burns said. "A fella named Wilkins, George Wilkins."

Chapter Forty-Two

Barbary Coast had a police station.

Apparently, the San Francisco police department had expanded since she had last been there. Luckily, she didn't have to go to the same station she'd gone to almost five years ago.

She'd had to bite her tongue when Rex Burns told her the dead man was a vet named George Wilkins. And she'd had to have sex with him one more time before he allowed her to go to her room.

"You'll have to get breakfast on your own today," he told her. "I have things to do."

"No problem," she said. "Thanks for a lovely evening."

"Thank you," he said, "we'll have to do it again, soon."

Knowing his reputation with women, she wondered if he meant that—not that it really mattered to her. She'd hoped to see something in his living quarters that might offer some information about whether or not he was involved with the shanghaiing, but found nothing. If he was involved, he was too smart to have anything out where it could be seen.

But she could worry about that later. In her room she got dressed in one of her simplest frocks—which happened to be blue—and left the saloon. She was hungry, but first she wanted more information on what had happened to Wilkins. Having no idea where the police station was, she split the difference. She stopped in a café just off the Barbary Coast to have breakfast, and then asked the elderly waiter if he knew the way to the police station. He was happy to give her directions.

When she found the station, it was a brick building with a sign out front that read BARBARY COAST STATION. Inside, she found one of those big front desks she had seen last time she was in San Francisco. The man behind it watched as she approached, looking her up and down. He was in his forties, young enough to appreciate her.

"Can I help you, Ma'am?"

"I hope so," she said. "I want to talk to someone about George Wilkins."

"And what about him?"

"He's dead."

The man looked surprised. "When did that happen?"

"Look," she said, "I heard he was killed last night on the docks. I work at the Blue Lady Saloon, and some of your men were there talking to Mr. Burns about it."

"Our men? You mean, detectives?"

"Yes," she said, "detectives."

"Well, I don't know anythin' about what those fellas do," he said. "Why don't you have a seat and lemme find out?"

There were some benches along the walls, and she chose one and sat. She wasn't there very long when a man came out, looked around, spotted her and came over. He was tall, thin, looked something like a ferret, was probably 50. His clothes looked as if they had been slept in.

"I'm Detective Jaden. You know something about George Wilkins gettin' murdered?" he asked.

"No," she said, standing, "but I knew him, and I was wondering what happened."

"How did you hear about the killing, Ma'am?"

"I work in the Blue Lady," she said. "Word got around in there."

"Uh-huh," he said. "Did you see him in there yesterday?"

"Well . . ." she wasn't sure what she wanted to say about that.

"I tell you what," he said, before she could answer. "Come on in the back with me where we can talk more comfortably."

"Uh, well, all right."

He led her around that big desk, across the floor to a hallway. He led her down that hall to a small office.

"Have a seat," he said, sitting behind the desk in the room. She didn't know if this was his office or not. It looked too neat.

"My partner and me, we were at the Blue Lady this mornin', talkin' to your boss, Burns."

"That was what I heard."

"First," he said, picking up a pencil so he could take notes, "what's your name?"

Okay, how should she answer that. Since she was secretly working for the Pinkertons, she figured she should stay that person, for now.

"Rachel Dolan."

"And how did you know Wilkins?"

"I met him over four years ago, here in San Francisco."

"Met him?"

"He took care of my horse."

"So it was business?"

"Just business," she said.

"And at that time were you working at the Blue Lady?"

"No, I was just passing through."

"And how long have you been back?"

"It's under four weeks, since I started working at the Blue Lady."

"Okay." He wrote something down, then seemed to dot a bunch of "i's" before looking up at her.

"Did you see Wilkins at the Blue Lady yesterday?" he asked. "Nobody can seem to tell us that. Not Burns, and not the bartender, Wood . . . Wood . . . something."

"Woodbury."

"That's it." He wrote again, presumably that name. There were no "i's" to dot. "So . . . was he there?"

"He was there, but not last night," she said. "He came in early in the day."

"To gamble? Drink? For a poke?"

"I don't take men upstairs for that, and Mr. Wilkins didn't go up with another girl. He just had a beer, and we talked."

"About old times?"

"Something like that."

"He didn't say what he was doing on the docks?"

"He said there were animals on the docks that needed help," she said.

"Anything else?"

"Yes," she said, "he told me he was going to come back in the evening."

Detective Jaden looked up at her from his notes.

"He said he was coming back?"

"That's right."

"Did he say why? Who he was going to see?"

"Well . . . he said he wanted to come back and see me in a more revealing gown."

Jaden stared at her for a few moments, then made more notes.

"Did he say he knew Rex Burns?"

"No, he didn't."

"Had you ever seen Wilkins and Burns together?"

"No," she said. "This was the one and only day I saw Wilkins."

"And he didn't talk to anyone else?"

"He spoke to the bartender."

Jaden wrote something else down, then looked off into the distance.

"All right," he said. "That's all."

"I'm sorry," she said, "but that's not all."

"Yes?"

"I came here to find out how he died."

"He was killed," Jaden said, "beaten to death."

"Oh my God," she said. "What with?"

"Something blunt," he said. "A club, a stick, something we figure you'd find on the docks."

"That's awful," she said. "He was such a nice man."

"Was he?"

"Well . . . when I knew him, he was. Had that changed?"

"We believe he was involved in some sort of criminal activity, which probably got him killed," Jaden said.

"So why would you ask if he knew Rex Burns?"

"Mr. Burns may be your boss," Jaden said, 'but we believe he is also involved in criminal activities, especially on the docks."

"Like what?" she asked. "Not . . . shanghaiing people."

"Shanghai?" Jaden repeated. "That's not even against the law. Why would you ask about that? Is Rex Burns involved in a shanghaiing ring?"

"I—I have no idea,' she said, quickly. "I was just . . . that's just the kind of thing you hear about on the docks . . . isn't it?"

"Sure," Jaden said, "that . . . and murder."

Chapter Forty-Three

Roxy left the police station with more questions than answers.

Had George Wilkins become a criminal over the years?

Was he involved with Rex Burns?

Was Burns a criminal? Or worse, a killer?

She went back to the Blue Lady, wanting to get in touch with Sam Warren, but not knowing how. As she walked in the batwing doors the place was just starting to get busy with early drinkers and gamblers and, among them, standing at the bar, was Warren.

She couldn't walk right up and talk to him. She wasn't dressed for work, and stopping at the bar to talk to a customer might look suspicious.

When he saw her, he made as if he was going to pick up his beer and walk over to her, but she quickly shook her head. She went directly to the stairs and hurried up to her room to dress. The only problem was, she wasn't scheduled to start for hours. How would it look for her to be in among the customers on her own time? She was going to have to take that chance.

She came back down in a very revealing green dress, shoulders and breasts very much on display.

When she got downstairs she saw Lil and Mona working the floor. Lil gave her a smile, but Mona scowled, wondering what she was doing there so early. Roxy ignored the girl and walked over to the bar, where Sam Warren was still standing.

"Did anyone get shanghaied last night?" she asked him, immediately.

"Yeah, they did," Warren said. "That's why Pinkerton sent me here." He kept his voice down.

"I need to see him," she said. "I might have something for him."

"Well, good," he said. "When and where?"

"Tonight . . . at that fleabag hotel I was staying in when I first got to town."

"Fleabag?"

"He'll know what I mean."

"What time?'

"Midnight," she said. "If I'm late, tell him to just wait."

"So whataya know—"

"Just go!"

He took one more sip of his beer, put it down unfinished, turned and left.

"What is it with you and that runt?" Mona asked, coming up behind her.

"He likes me," Roxy said.

"Why are you here?" Mona asked. "You ain't supposed to work until later."

"I'm not working," Roxy told her. "I'm just killing time."

"Well, kill it somewhere else," Mona said. "It's bad enough I gotta compete with you when we're workin' the same hours."

"You know what?" Roxy said. "You won't have to compete with me today, at all. If Rex is looking for me tell him I felt sick and went to see a doctor."

"Sick?" Mona asked.

"I'll see you later," she said, cutting Mona off.

She went to the stairs, hurried up to her room and changed her clothes, again. When she came out she hoped she wouldn't run into Rex Burns—or anybody, for that matter, but on her way to the batwing doors Lil stopped her.

"Mona says you're sick," the little blonde said. "What's the matter?"

"I've got a headache I can't get rid of," Roxy said. "I'll be back later, but if I'm late for work make an excuse for me with Wood or Burns. Okay?"

"Sure, Rach, sure," Lil said. "Feel better!" she added, as Roxy went out the doors.

Chapter Forty-Four

Warren was on his way to deliver her message to Robert Pinkerton, but Roxy had decided she needed to see him sooner. Also, she'd forgotten to ask Sam Warren a question.

She assumed he would go to Pinkerton's office on Market Street with her message. She decided to wait outside the building and see if one of them came out. She was once again wearing her more sedate dress, and since she wouldn't have been able to wear the thigh holster with it, she could have chosen to bring her derringer. But she had a small, drawstring purse she'd bought while shopping, just for this purpose. Her special Colt fit right inside of it. So she was properly armed for whatever happened.

She watched the five-story building that housed the office of The Pinkerton Detective Agency for about half-an-hour before Sam Warren came out. He looked around nervously, fidgeted a bit before choosing a direction in which to walk. Roxy stepped from her doorway and followed. It was not her intention to tail him, she simply wanted to catch up to him somewhere they could talk in private. In the end she rushed up behind him and shoved him into a doorway.

"What the—oh, it's you. Whataya doin' here?"

"I changed my mind," she said. "I want to talk to Robert right away, but I don't want to be seen going into his building."

"I just came from there!" he complained.

"I know," she said. "Go back and tell him to meet me at that hotel now."

"Now?"

"Right now!"

"Okay, okay," Sam Warren said. "Jeez, I can't wait til this is over."

As he ran back to the Pinkerton's building, Roxy thought she felt the same way.

***

Roxy forgot that the Flamingo Rose was not only a flea-bag, but a tacky looking one.

She waited in the lobby, sitting on a rickety wooden bench, for about half an hour before Robert Pinkerton appeared.

"We have to talk—" she said, standing, but he cut her off by taking her arm.

"Not here," he said. "Even this is too public. Besides, this is just the type of hotel Barbary Coast types would frequent."

She hadn't thought of that, and felt stupid for it.

He led her out to the street, then turned left.

"We could have met at my house," he said, "but that's too far, now."

"Sorry," she said, "I felt I shouldn't be seen there."

"Probably right," he said. "Okay, look, there's a small saloon. Let's go in there."

They crossed the street and entered. Luckily, it was deserted but for the bartender. He looked happy when they walked in, and annoyed when Pinkerton ordered two coffees. The detective carried them to a back table, where they both sat.

"All right, what's going on."

"Do you remember me telling you about my first trip here?" she asked. "The night we . . . spent together."

"Yes," he said, "you told me something about a vet, and some horse people."

"Right, well, the vet's name was George Wilkins," she said, "and last night he was killed on the docks."

"So?"

"He came to the Blue Lady first," she said. "We saw each other there—"

"Did he give you away?"

"No," she said, "but we talked, and he was supposed to be coming back last night. I believe he was on his way there when he was killed."

"Okay, I heard something about this," he said. "He was bludgeoned?"

"Beaten to death," she said, assuming that was what "bludgeoned" meant.

Pinkerton looked thoughtful.

"What is it?"

"Well, when they shanghai somebody they do it one of two ways," he said. "Either they Mickey Finn their drinks—that's a drug—or they bash them over the head."

"You think somebody was trying to shanghai him?"

"Maybe, but why not wait until he got to the Blue Lady?"

"That's something I wanted to talk to you about," she said. "I don't think the shanghaiing is being done from the Blue Lady."

"What?"

"I talked to Rex about it—"

"Rex?"

"Rex Burns, the owner," she said. "He really doesn't like that some people refer to his place as 'the Shanghai Saloon.'"

"Did you tell him that?"

"No, he told me," she said. "he says if it was going on in his saloon, he'd know."

"Damn right, he'd know," Pinkerton said, "because he's the head honcho."

"Did Sam tell you about the two men?"

"What two men?"

"The two men who sit under Zack."

"What the hell is a Zack?" Pinkerton asked.

Patiently, Roxy told him about the two well-dressed men who sat under the painting called "Zachariah."

"And they were there last night."

"What's that got to do with anything?" he asked.

"I think they've been there each night somebody got shanghaied," she said.

"You think they have something to do with it?"

"I think they may be using the Blue Lady, and Rex knows nothing about it."

Pinkerton thought about it for a moment, then shook his head.

191

"Look, we have it on good authority that Rex Burns is sharp," he said. "How sharp could he be if this was being done under his nose and he didn't know about it?"

"What if he just doesn't want to know?" she asked.

"You mean he's turning a blind eye?" Pinkerton asked. "That doesn't make him much better."

"Not deliberately," she said.

"You sound like you're trying to make excuses for him," Pinkerton said. "Is something happening between the two of you?"

"I'm going to pretend you didn't say that," she said.

"I just mean, I've heard he has a reputation with women—"

"Even if I did have sex with him," she said, cutting him off, "don't you think I'm capable of doing that and staying in control of myself?"

She stared at him, daring him to say something about it.

"Okay, let's forget that," he said. "Why didn't you send word to me about these two men before?"

"I did," she said. "In fact, I asked Sam Warren to tell you early on, and then I asked him again to find out what he could about them."

"Sam never said a word."

"Can you trust him?"

He rubbed his jaw. "I thought I could."

"He does seem nervous all the time."

"I thought that was just his manner," Pinkerton said. "Talk about someone being taken in—I'll check on him. And I'll look into the murder of this vet."

"And another thing," she said. "I talked to the detective from the police department. His name was . . . Jaden. Looks like a ferret."

"I know him."

"He thinks George Wilkins was up to something illegal."

"The vet?"

"When I knew him he was a vet," she said, "but that was over four years ago."

"All right," Pinkerton said, "I'll have to check on that, too."

"But check on Sam Warren first," she said.

"I'd hate to think he's been taking me fir a fool," Pinkerton said. "My old man would never let me hear the end of it."

"Then let's not tell him," Roxy suggested.

Chapter Forty-Five

As they left the saloon Pinkerton asked, "Where are you headed?"

"Back to the Blue Lady," she said. "I didn't know how long it would take me to get to you, but I still have plenty of time to get to work."

"All right," he said, "but keep your eye out. I'm still not convinced that the Blue Lady isn't smack in the middle of this."

"I'll watch it."

"Did you come out unarmed?"

She gave him a light smack with her string purse, letting him feel the weight of the gun inside.

"I should've known better," he said. "I'll be in touch."

***

When Roxy got back to the Blue Lady it was doing its usual midday business. She made her way through the crowd to the stairs and up to her room.

Inside she sat in front of her mirror to get ready for work, but paused a moment to consider. If Rex Burns was totally innocent, but his place was being used by those two men who sat under Zack, then what did they do when they came in. For all she could see they sat, drank, hardly talked to each other, let alone interact with other customers, or even the girls.

And then there was Sam Warren. Was Pinkerton's inside man actually "inside?" Was his shaky appearance an act, or was he nervous for good reason?

There was a knock on her door as she was working on her hair. Lil would have walked right in.

"Yes?"

"It's Rex."

"Come on in."

He opened the door and entered, wearing one of his black suits.

"Lil told me you were sick. I wanted to check in on you. Are you all right?"

"I'm fine," she said, touching her temple. "Headaches. The doctor gave me some kind of powder. I'm not even sure I'm going to use it."

"As long as you're all right," he said. He sat on the bed, and as he did his hand hit the string purse she had left there. "What the—" He picked up the purse. "What's this?"

"Just what ladies carry in their purses when they go walking alone," she explained.

He opened it and took out the Colt that had been specially constructed for her by the Gunsmith.

"You know how to use this?"

"Pretty well, actually," she admitted.

He hefted the gun for a moment, then put it back in the purse.

"Why do I get the feeling you're not what you seem?" he asked.

She stood up, put her hands on her hips.

"And what do I seem to be?"

"A young woman working beneath her," he said.

"You have that low an opinion of your own place?" she asked.

"Oh no," he said, "I know exactly what this place is. I think I just have that high an opinion of you."

"I'm just one of the girls, Rex."

He stood up.

"Nobody believes that, Rachel," he said, "not even the girls."

As he started to leave the room she said, "Rex, the man who was killed last night was a vet named Wilkins. Did you know him?"

"Wilkins?" he shrugged. "Not unless he was a customer here. I don't have much need of a vet, Rachel. Have a good night working."

He left, closing the door gently behind him.

***

Even more than before Rex Burns thought that Rachel Dolan was something other than what she appeared to be. What he had to decide was whether or not that something was a threat to him.

Rather than go to his office, he turned and went up to his living quarters.

***

She hurriedly took the gun from the purse, attached the holster to her thigh and slid the gun home. Lowering her skirts, she felt much better. When the gun was in Rex's hands, she was anything but comfortable. If he suspected she was something other than what she was, he might have made use of the gun. More now than ever she felt he was nothing but a businessman, and the word "shanghai" was not part of his business.

Maybe it was time to confide in him. Maybe if she told him what she was really doing there, and what was going on, he'd want to cooperate, but if she did that, she might be putting her life in danger. Before she did that, she was going to have to be dead sure of him.

Chapter Forty-Six

Roxy worked a few hours before things started to happen.

She was picking up drinks from Wood at the bar when the two entered in and walked to the table beneath Zachariah. That was when she realized that nobody else ever sat there. Did everyone in the place know to leave that table empty for these two men?

"Wood," she said, as he set drinks on her tray, "who are those two guys?"

He looked to see who she was pointing at, then said, "Don't worry about it, Rachel. Just come back here so you can keep delivering their drinks to them."

That suited her, she wanted another close look at them.

She delivered the beer she was carrying, went back to Wood to get the two men their Jasper Hole whiskey, then carried it over to them. She did her bending over thing as she set the glasses in front of them.

"Nice to see you boys again," she said, keeping her voice low and sexy.

"Thank you," one of them said, reaching for his drink.

"You know," she said, "I notice you fellas never pay for your drinks. Are you friends with of the owner? Or do you own a piece of this place yourselves?"

Both men looked up at her, as if seeing her for the first time.

"Go away," one of them said.

"But—"

"Have someone else bring the bottle," the other man said.

"Fine," she said, acting insulted.

She went back to the bar where Wood was waiting.

"Those men are rude!" she complained.

"Did you talk to them?"

"I tried to—"

"I should've told you not to talk to them," he said, cutting her off. "They don't like it."

"Why not?"

"He shrugged. "Who knows?"

"Then why do they come here?"

"To drink, I suppose."

"They don't even talk to each other."

"Maybe," Woodbury said, "they don't like each other. Here, bring them the bottle."

"No," she said, "they asked that somebody else bring the bottle."

"Fine," he said, "I'll have Mona do it."

As Mona went over with the bottle, Roxy was surprised again when Robert Pinkerton walked in. She recognized him, even though he was dressed like a longshoreman.

He went directly to the bar, ordered a beer and then looked over at her. Then he said something to Woodbury, who came down the bar to Roxy.

"Fella over there wants the pleasure of your company," the big, black bartender said.

"Did you tell him I don't take fellas upstairs?"

"He said it was just for a drink."

"Okay, then."

She sashayed along the bar, avoiding grabbing hands, until she reached Pinkerton's side.

"What the hell are you doing here?" she asked him, smiling.

He waited while the bartender brought a beer over for Roxy, and then walked away.

"You were right about Warren, and those two," he said to her. "Once Warren broke, I had him contact them."

"He was working with them?" Roxy nodded toward the large painting.

"Oh, yes," Pinkerton said. "That was our problem. Putting a nothing like Warren together with these men."

"And who are they?"

"Ship owners," Pinkerton said. "Basically, these are men who would normally hire us. We didn't expect that actual owners would be behind the shanghaiing. The one on the right is Albert Dillon, and the other one is Lewis Foreman."

"So how do you prove it?"

"They're here to meet with their inside contact," Pinkerton said, "only the inside contact doesn't know it. That means somebody around here is very puzzled by their appearance again so soon."

"Wasn't Warren their contact?"

"Warren was their intermediary," Pinkerton said.

"All of these terms are confusing," she admitted. "I just want to know who's guilty."

"We're going to find that out tonight," he said, with confidence.

"And where's Warren?" she asked. "Won't he give you away?"

"We're holding him," Pinkerton said. "Let's just drink our beers and watch."

That's what they did, all the time smiling and pretending to be flirting.

"Who brought them the bottle?" Pinkerton asked.

"I brought them their first drinks," she said "I tried to get them to talk and they told me to go away. Then Mona brought the bottle."

"Which one's Mona?"

"The tall one, there."

"Nice," Pinkerton said, with approval. "Did she talk to them?"

"Not a word."

"Hmmm. Did you ever see Warren talk to them?"

"No," she said, "but that doesn't mean he didn't. I never really watched him closely. And I guess he could've met them just outside."

"So who did Warren talk to when he came in?"

"Only two people," she said. "Me, and Woodbury, the bartender."

"The bartender!" Pinkerton said.

"It couldn't be Wood," she said.

They both looked over at the bartender, who was pouring drinks, but whose attention seemed to be on the two ship owners sitting underneath Zack. He looked confused.

"He's waiting for Warren," Pinkerton said. "He can't send them a message without him."

"Oh Jesus," Roxy said, "Woodbury? This'll kill Burns."

"Where is the owner, by the way?"

"Either upstairs, or in his office," she said.

"Did those two ever bring anyone with them?" Pinkerton asked.

"Not that I've seen," she said, "but that doesn't mean they don't have men planted in here ahead of time."

"Well," Pinkerton said, "they wouldn't be the only ones."

"You have somebody planted here?"

Pinkerton smiled at her over his mug. "I have you, don't I?"

Chapter Forty-Seven

While they watched all three men—Woodbury and the two ship owners—seemed to get antsy.

"They're wondering what's going on," Pinkerton said, "and they're looking for Warren."

"They need their—what did you call it?"

"Intermediary."

"Yes," she said, pushing away from the bar, "maybe they should get a new one."

"Rox—" he started to call, but didn't want to give her real name away.

She walked across the room—bumped, jostled and grabbed at a time or two—until she reached their table. The two men looked up at her.

"I thought we asked—" one of them started, but she cut him off.

"If you're waiting for Warren he's not coming," she said.

"What?" the other one asked. The two men exchanged a glance.

"I'm taking his place," she went on.

"Who says?" the first man asked.

"Wood," she said. "If you don't believe me, go and ask him."

The one thing they never did was go to the bar to talk to Woodbury.

"You're Foreman," she said, "and you're Dillon. I'm Rachel."

The two men looked around the room nervously.

"It's okay," she said, "have one of your men go and talk to Wood."

"Our men?" Dillon asked.

"Come on," she said, "you wouldn't ever come in here without somebody watching your backs."

"You seem to know a lot about what we would or wouldn't do," Foreman said.

"Well, that should tell you something," she said.

They seemed to think it over, and then Foreman said, "No."

Dillon said, "Go away."

"I'll give you a few minutes to consider it," she told them, and went back to the bar.

"What happened?" Pinkerton asked.

"I think I scared them."

As they watched, Foreman abruptly waved his hand in the air. Suddenly, four men moved out from the crowd and closed in on Roxy.

"You better move," she told Pinkerton.

"Not a chance."

It looked like she scared the two ship owners so much they wanted her killed. The action spread quickly through the crowd, and men started to hit the deck.

Rex Burns came down the stairs and, seeing most of his customers on the floor, said, "What the hell—"

Roxy was already pulling the hem of her dress up-as the four men went for their guns.

Pinkerton pulled a small gun from a shoulder holster.

At the sound of the first shot, everything began to move quickly.

Roxy got her hand on the butt of her Colt and yanked it free, tearing the dress so that her thigh was now exposed.

As the four men started to fire she reached out with one hand and pushed Pinkerton aside. With her other hand she started to fire.

Woodbury pulled a club from beneath the bar and raised it, intending to strike Roxy—or "Rachel"—with it. Pinkerton shot him.

Roxy fired quickly, two shots, and two of the men spun and went down. But the petticoats had kept her from getting the gun out fast enough. The other two men were firing. In their haste, however, their shots went wide. They struck Roxy, but one glanced off her bare right shoulder, and the other creased her bare left upper arm.

She squatted quickly and fired again . . . and again . . .

The third shot struck one of the men in the throat. He dropped his gun wrapped both his hands around the wound, and died.

The fourth shot hit the remaining man in the chest. Rather than spinning him as had happened with the first two men, it simply shoved him back two steps, where he stopped, shocked, dropped his gun, and then fell on it.

The two ship builders rose from their seats and headed for the door.

"Not a chance!" Rex Burns shouted. He had already been moving, and quickly got between them and the door, showing them his gun.

In the time it took Roxy to fire four times, Pinkerton had gotten off only one shot, but it kept Woodbury from braining her with the club. He was leaning back against the liquor shelves, holding his arm, blood seeping from between his fingers.

Roxy stood up, gun in hand, shapely right thigh and long leg in plain sight.

Rex Burns shouted, "Somebody better tell me what the hell is goin' on!"

Chapter Forty-Eight

"Rachel Dolan" was gone.

She was Roxy Doyle again.

She was sitting in Robert Pinkerton's office, waiting for him.

"I'm sorry to keep you waiting," he said, hurrying in and sitting behind his desk.

"That's all right," she said. "Are you satisfied?"

"Oh yes," he said. "it's taken a few days, but we've got it closed down. And Rex Burns was not involved, as you said. It was his bartender Woodbury, Sam Warren, and Foreman and Dillon, the ship owners."

"But I'm sure Rex is very upset."

"To say the least," Pinkerton said. "He thinks himself a total idiot for not seeing what was going on. Can't say I disagree with him."

"That's not fair."

"Maybe not. How are you feeling?"

"I'm fine." She was dressed in her trail clothes, again, her gun strapped to her hip. Both of her wounds had been superficial, and were bandaged.

"Well, here you go," he said, passing her an envelope.

She opened it and looked inside. It was a bank draft for the amount they had agreed on.

"You can go right to our bank here in town," he said. "You won't have any trouble getting the money."

"Thank you," she said.

"No, it's I who's grateful, to you and to Clint Adams for recommending you."

"I think we've forgotten one thing."

"No," he said, "I have all the information you gave me about your father right here." He tapped the top of his desk. "Stay in touch with me, and I'll give you anything we uncover that might lead to his whereabouts."

"I appreciate that," she said, "but I was also talking about George Wilkins. What happened with him? Was he involved?"

"Not that we or the police could discover," Pinkerton said. "He was in the wrong place at the wrong time. He was dressed too well to be walking on the Barbary Coast. He'd been cleaned out, so it looks like a robbery and a killing. Just another Barbary Coast story."

"All right, then . . ." she said, sadly. She couldn't help feeling a slight sense of responsibility, since he was returning to the Blue lady to see her. On the other hand, what had he been doing there in the first place? She decided not to dwell on it.

She stood up, and he did so, as well.

"Leaving San Francisco?" he asked.

"Soon," she said. "I'm going to stop back in at the Blue Lady. There are a couple of people I made friends with. I'd like to explain things to them and say goodbye."

They shook hands like business associates, the one night they had spent together forgotten, and she left his office.

***

Outside on the street she looked for a horse drawn cab to take her to the Barbary Coast. Before she could hail one, a carriage pulled up and the door opened. She found herself looking at Chief-of-Police Benjamin Anderson, looking much the same as the last time she saw him, just a little older.

"Get in!" he said.

"That's all right, I'll get a cab—"

"It wasn't an invitation."

"All right, then."

As she started to climb in he said, "Give my driver your destination."

"The Blue Lady Saloon," she told him, "on the Barbary Coast."

The man nodded.

She got in, sat across from the chief, and off they went. Anderson was wearing a uniform, with his hat on the seat next to him. He was also wearing a gun.

"I thought I told you never to come back to San Francisco," he said.

"That was almost five years ago, Chief," she said. "I'm a different person, now. I thought you might be, too."

"Well, I'm not," he said. "I'm the same person who didn't like that you killed three men last time, and I don't like it that you killed four men this time."

"I didn't plan it—"

"No, of course not," he said. "You probably never plan it, but it happens just the same."

"Look, I was asked to come here—"

"I know all about it," he said. "I've talked with Mr. Pinkerton."

"Then you know my job is finished and I'll be leaving."

"Yet you're going to the Barbary Coast."

"Just to say goodbye to some people," she said. "Don't worry, Chief. I'm leaving San Francisco today."

"Plan on coming back anytime soon?"

"No!"

"Then again," he said, "you didn't plan this visit, did you?"

"No, I didn't."

***

As she entered the Blue Lady she saw Lil standing behind the bar, wearing one of her more sedate dresses.

"There you are!" Lil said. "We've been wonderin' where you went?"

"I'm just here to say goodbye, Lil," Roxy said. "And to tell you my real name."

"Your real name? It's not Rachel?"

"No, it's Roxy, Roxy Doyle."

Lil smiled. "I like that better! But why did you need to change your name?"

"I'll let Rex tell you about that. Where is he?"

"In his office."

"I'm going to say goodbye to him, and then I'll be leaving San Francisco."

"Will you come back?"

"That's not the plan," Roxy said, "but you never know."

She went to the back wall and knocked on Rex Burns' door.

"Come!"

He looked up from his desk as she entered.

"There you are," he said. "Rachel?"

"Roxy," she said, "Doyle."

She could see that, unlike Lil, he recognized the name.

"I see."

"I'm here to say goodbye," she said, "and to tell you not to beat yourself up."

"That's kind of hard not to do," he said. "I put a lot of trust in Woodbury."

"I guess," she said, "it took that kind of trust to pull the wool over your eyes."

"Well, I can guarantee you one thing," he said. "It won't happen again."

"I'm sure it won't. Goodbye, Rex."

"Uh . . ."

"Yes?"

"Talking about things that might happen again?" He raised his eyebrows. "I have some time now."

She smiled.

"Unfortunately, that's something else that's never going to happen again."

Coming October 2017

Lady Gunsmith 4
Roxy Doyle and the Traveling Circus Show

By
AWARD-WINNING AUTHOR
J.R. Roberts

For more information
visit: www.speakingvolumes.us

Now Available

Lady Gunsmith 2
A New Adult Western Series

Here Lies Roxy Doyle, Lady Gunsmith
shot to death in Sunset, New Mexico.

By
AWARD-WINNING AUTHOR
J.R. Roberts

For more information
visit: www.speakingvolumes.us

ANGEL EYES *series*
by
Award-Winning Author
Robert J. Randisi (J.R. Roberts)

Visit us at www.speakingvolumes.us

TRACKER *series*
by
Award-Winning Author
Robert J. Randisi (J.R. Roberts)

Visit us at www.speakingvolumes.us

MOUNTAIN JACK PIKE *series*
by
Award-Winning Author
Robert J. Randisi (J.R. Roberts)

Visit us at www.speakingvolumes.us

Sign up for free and bargain books

Join the Speaking Volumes mailing list

Text

ILOVEBOOKS

to 22828 to get started.